William Pember Reeves

Canterbury rhymes

Second Edition

William Pember Reeves

Canterbury rhymes
Second Edition

ISBN/EAN: 9783337259631

Printed in Europe, USA, Canada, Australia, Japan

Cover: Foto ©Andreas Hilbeck / pixelio.de

More available books at **www.hansebooks.com**

CANTERBURY RHYMES.

SECOND EDITION:

WITH NOTES AND AN APPENDIX.

EDITED BY W. P. REEVES.

CHRISTCHURCH:
PRINTED BY THE "LYTTELTON TIMES" COMPANY LIMITED, GLOUCESTER STREET.
1883.

PREFACE TO THE SECOND EDITION.

An American author, in introducing, the other day, a new book to the Public, commenced his Preface with the remark, that his volume had *not* been published "in deference to the urgent and repeated requests of the writer's enthusiastic friends, who must therefore be responsible,"—and so forth. He had written it, he went on to explain, to please himself, and he published it with the hope of making a little money out of it. The publishers of the present edition of the *Canterbury Rhymes* wish they could imitate the candour and share the hopes of that author. Unfortunately they can do neither the one nor the other. To say nothing of the latter, it happens to be true that during the fifteen years in which the original edition has been out of print, suggestions have often been made to them to print another. Indeed, it is to the persuasions of a genial old identity that this volume owes its existence; and to the same gentleman's courtesy the Editor is indebted for the copy of the original *Rhymes* used in preparing the present edition. On going through the old contributions, it seemed advisable not to reproduce a few of them, and nine were therefore excised. The others are reprinted unaltered, and the orginal Notes, written by the late Mr. Crosbie Ward, have also been left untouched; any additions which it has been thought necessary to make to them are carefully marked by brackets, thus [ ].

As will be seen, the old *Rhymes*, which, by the way, were nearly all reprints from the *Lyttelton Times*, are signed with the initials of their authors. Considering the lapse of time since their first appearance, there would seem now no valid reason for preserving even this amount of anonymity, and the curious reader may therefore be at once told the names for which the letters stand. J. E. F-G. represent James Edward FitzGerald, Canterbury's first Superintendent; C. W., Crosbie Ward; E. J. W., Edward Jerningham Wakefield; J., the present Dean of Christchurch; S. R., Sarah, the first wife of the Rev. John Raven; G. C., Canon Cotterill; J. T. R., Dr. Rouse of Lyttelton; W. J. S., William Jukes Steward, now M.H.R. for Waimate. It may be mentioned that the preface to the first edition came from the same pen to which we owe the Notes and what is brightest and most amusing in the *Rhymes* themselves.

Of the Appendix, it is enough to say, that more than half has been taken from the *Canterbury Punch* of 1864-65; this was edited by Mr. Ward, and his hand may be traced in several of the ballads and skits reprinted from it here. The other selections have mostly been chosen from the *Lyttelton Times* and *Canterbury Times*, while the "Lay of a Lost Spec," with which the series concludes, and which it is hoped will show that Canterbury Rhymsters have not altogether lost their cunning in these days, came out, as may be remembered, in the *Press*, last year.

The Editor of this little Volume has not much to say of it by way of explanation or apology. Critical readers, who find that some of the *Rhymes* have perhaps no great amount of intrinsic poetical value, will remember that the work does not profess to make its appearance on the strength of poetical merit alone. The *Rhymes* were written in Canterbury for Canterbury readers, and their best claim to favour on their own soil will be found in the old associations connected with them, and in the pleasant, unpretending record they form of the amusements, quarrels, politics, and progress of Provincial Canterbury. As men go down from generation to generation, and

"One hands on to another the burning torch of existence,"

there is something else to be handed on in the shape of such memorials as can be collected of peculiar traits of each passing age. To give a fair notion of what life was in Canterbury's earlier days, is not perhaps so easy as either those who lived it or their successors may imagine. It differed far more from the existing order of things than the present is likely to do from the immediate future. The pilgrim was not only quite another man from those who have followed him: he was also a colonist of a stamp distinct in many respects from any other class of pioneer in Australasia. He had his failings, of course; but those who take the trouble to read these *Rhymes* will see that he had a brighter side; will recognise what they have been told—that the Founders of Canterbury were English gentlemen and gentlewomen, in the fullest sense of those much-abused words; and will not be ungrateful to those who, though now themselves fast disappearing, have left enduring marks of good work behind them.

PREFACE TO THE FIRST EDITION.

This little book, the compilation of which has been undertaken with the hope of aiding in a work of charity, has no pretentions to the title of a Book of Poetry. It is merely a collection of rhymes, chiefly of a humorous character, which have been written and first published in Canterbury. Almost all which appeared in the earlier days of the settlement are reprinted here, for the sake of the old associations which attach to them. But comparatively few have been selected out of the large number of newspaper verses which later years have produced.

Wherever it has been possible to ascertain the Author's name, initials have been appended to the verses, so that the reader may understand how many different hands have contributed to the 'Poet's Corner' in Canterbury, and may be able to account for the great variety in the style of composition and the subjects chosen. It is not perhaps so easy to account for the disparaging language used so generally of the country, its climate and its people, their rulers, their manners, and their pursuits, unless we accept the solution that Canterbury is in every way so excellent that evil can only be spoken of the province in pure fun, as is the case in these pages.

No alterations of consequence have been made in the text from the first publication. A few words only have been changed, where a satirical remark has seemed to pass the boundary of good humoured license; or where, for some temporary purpose, the words as originally written had been altered on the first appearance in the newspapers, and have now been restored.

CONTENTS.

Night Watch Song of the Charlotte Jane ... ...
Canterbury Emigrant ... ...
English Labourer's Response ... ...
Pilgrims and Prophets ... ...
Lines on a Recent Calamity ... ...
Christchurch Colonists' Society ... ...
Shagroon's Lament ... ...
Overseer's Lament ... ...
Lay of the Last Registered Dog ... ...
Proclamation of the Manners and Customs of New Zealand ...
Canterbury in September, 1853... ... ...
"Greece is, where the Greeks are" ... ...
The Avon ... ...
A Historical Picture ... ...
Battle af Sinope ... ...
Tobacco ... ...
Charades on Unpopular Subjects--

No. 1—Bridle Path ... ...
No. 2—Rhymester ... ...
No. 3—Heathcote ... ...
No. 4—Tariff ... ...
No. 5—Railway ... ...
No. 6—Bullocks ... ...
No. 7—Lady Love ... ...
No. 8—Billow ... ...

Lay of the Sumner Road ... ...
Provincial Parodies—

No. 1—Railroadior ... ...
No. 2—The Struggle of Papanui ... ...
No. 3—Road Lines ... ...
No. 4—Town of Christchurch ... ...
No. 5—Ballad of the Ancient Member ... ...
No. 6—Song of the Squatters ... ...
No. 7—The Sumner Road ... ...

PAGE.
Address to the Provincial Council 53
Where's the Engineer 54
Epigram 55
Charade for the Times 56
Immigrant's Carol for Christmas 57
The Town and the Torrent 58
Ode to New Zealand 66
Album Lines; The Bazaar 69
Arcades Ambo 70
The First of May 72
Lament of Canterbury 74
The Lost Steamship 76
The Runaways 79
Song before Session 87
What does Lawyer Louis say? 90
Nursery Rhymes for Political Babies 92
Abridged Edition of New Zealand War 92
A Bequest on the Battlefield 92
Some of the Affecting Adventures of Poor Cock Canterbury 92
A Road Song 94
Essence of Provincial Council 94
Rolleston's Farewell 95
A Choice 95
The Husband's Excuse 97
The Cur and the Calf 97
Reminiscences 99
The Last Fly of Summer 101
Constable "E" 102
Charlotte Godley's Well 104
Song of the Cab Drivers 105
Commercial Summary for England 107
A Leave-taking 108
The Doctors' Dilemma 112
The Charge at Parihaka 115
The Lay of a Lost Spec ... 117
Notes 125

CANTERBURY RHYMES.

The Night Watch Song of the "Charlotte Jane."(1)

'TIS the first watch of the night, brothers,
And the strong wind rides the deep;
And the cold stars shining bright, brothers,
Their mystic courses keep.
Whilst our ship her path is cleaving
The flashing waters through,
Here's a health to the land we are leaving,
And the land we are going to!

First sadly bow the head, brothers,
In silence o'er the wine,
To the memory of the dead, brothers,
The fathers of our line.
Though their tombs may not receive us,
Far o'er the ocean blue,
Their spirits ne'er shall leave us
In the land we are going to.

Whilst yet sad memories move us,
A second cup we'll drain
To the manly hearts that love us
In our old homes o'er the main.
Fond arms that used to caress us,
Sweet smiles from eyes of blue,
Lips which no more may bless us,
In the land we are going to.

But away with sorrow now, brothers,
Fill the wine-cup to the brim!
Here's to all who'll swear the vow, brothers,
Of this our midnight hymn:—
That each man shall be a brother,
Who has joined our gallant crew;
That we'll stand by one another
In the land we are going to!

Fill again, before we part, brothers,
Fill the deepest draught of all,
To the loved ones of our hearts, brothers,
Who reward and share our toil.
From husbands and from brothers,
All honour be their due,—
The noble maids and mothers
Of the land we are going to!

The wine is at an end, brothers;
But ere we close our eyes,
Let a silent prayer ascend, brothers,
For our gallant enterprise.
Should our toil be all unblest, brothers,
Should ill-winds of fortune blow,
May we find God's haven of rest, brothers,
In the land we are going to!

J. E. F-G.

"*Charlotte Jane,*" *Nov.* 2, 1850.

The Canterbury Emigrant.

(A new Edition of the "Irish Emigrant.")

I'M thinking of the day, Mary,
When we stood side by side,
Poor wanderers from our native land,
When first you were my bride.

The fern was waving tall and rank,
  And the wind blew keen and high,
But a smile was on your lip, Mary,
  And the love-light in your eye.

The place is greatly changed, Mary,
  The tall fern waves no more,
And many an Old World blossom bright
  Now nestles round our door.
Our home is snug and warm, Mary,
  As any Old World home,
And I prize its low thatched cottage roof
  More than a gilded dome.

Put a fresh log on the hearth, Mary,
  And call our friends around,
We'll celebrate our 'coming day,
  And the blessings we have found.
We journeyed forth in faith and hope,
  From our home across the main;
And now we are so happy here,
  We'd not go back again.

But we'll not forget the Old World,
  In boasting of the New,
Nor the many friends we left behind,
  The friends both kind and true.
We'll drink prosperity to all;
  And if they love good cheer,
And cannot find it where they are,
  Why, let them all come here!

April, 1851.

The English Labourer's Response to the song of the "Canterbury Emigrant."

I'VE heard your lay of hope and love;
I like its cheery tone;
And emulate the honest toil
By which your joys have grown:
I've toiled, with a tenacious faith,
For many a weary year,
But see no independence rise
My autumn days to cheer.

'Tis not that on your southern home
A brighter sun has smiled;
Or that my mother-country's soil
Will not support her child;
But when I echo back your song,
And towards New Zealand turn,
I feel that there they value *men*,
And native worth discern.

I dread lest these my children should
Those bitter feelings know
That from the rich man's scorn result,
Or from oppression grow;
Although Old England is endeared
By many ties to me,
Ere they shall bite the dust I'll seek
A home beyond the sea.

And so I gather up my flowers,
Before their brightness fades.
Thank God no broken law enchains,
No conscious thought upbraids!
Amid these 'low-thatched cottage roofs'
Our future home we'll raise,
And by God's blessing earn respect,
And happy 'coming' days.

May, 1851.

Pilgrims and Prophets. ([2])

Air—"Gaily the Troubadour."

GAILY the pilgrim harnessed his plough,
When he had built up a roof o'er his head;
Singing, "From Albion hither I come;
"Land of mine! land of mine! grow me some bread."

Proudly the prophet flourished his crook,
When he had landed his sheep from the west;
Singing, "From Philipland hither I come;
"Silly men! silly men! wool pays the best."

Quickly the prophet bred up his flock,
As he defied dogs, scab, and catarrh;
Singing, "To Philipland back I shall go,
"When they no longer need 'baccy and tar."

Slowly the pilgrim toiled for his crop,
And soon he sent golden wheat to the mill;
Singing, "For ever shall this be my shop;
"Shepherd-man! Shepherd-man! go if you will!"

Shortly the pilgrim and prophet agreed
The plough and the crook couldn't live far apart;
Singing, "Together we'll tend and we'll till;
"Shepherd-man! Farmer-man! keep a good heart!"

Lastly, the good men avoided a "smash,"
Whether to shear or to reap was their aim;
Singing, with cheers from the plains to the hills,
"Pilgrim! and prophet! be one and the same!"

August, 1851.

Lines on a Recent Calamity. ([3])

NO deep funereal bell—
No pageantry of woe—
No plumed hearse be here to tell
The "grief that passeth show."

Such signs by others treasured,
May force the added tear;
For *him* our mourning is not measured
By day, or month, or year.

His mem'ry need not plead
For the fame by others sought;
For kindly was his every deed,
And genial every thought.

Of his home no grudger he,
Of hand, or heart, or mind;
A very prodigal in sympathy
For the sorrows of his kind

To the near and dear, relief
Comes in guileless words and plain;
For the cause of *their* unending grief
Is *his* unmeasured gain!

But yet, methinks, *below*
Some monument there needs,
That ages yet unborn may know
And emulate his deeds.

Sculptured pile and dome—
Build with what art you can—
I like not these; they come not home,
Nor represent the MAN.

Join then! a work construct,
With GOOD for ages rife;
Such might posterity instruct—
Fit symbol of his LIFE!

September, 1851.

Christchurch Colonists' Society.

An Elaboration of the Information desired respecting the Restoration of the Excavation in the Market-place, Christchurch, to its original elevation.—Deliberation I.

IN the Market-place at Christchurch was made an excavation;
The gravel taken thence being used for reparation
Of the Heathcote Ferry-road, then in great dilapidation.
The Colonists' Society, desiring information,
Resolved on Tuesday last, after due deliberation,
That the Secretary do put himself into communication
With Mr. Godley, resident agent of the Association,
And request of him to answer, without prevarication,
If he at present purposes to effect a restoration
Of the Market-place at Christchurch to its original elevation.

It was strongly represented then that the preservation
Of the people's limbs and lives from such a situation
As that in which they find themselves, if through precipitation
They tumbled into, head over heels, said recited excavation,
Was a question which merited their first consideration.
That dirty roads and dark nights were sufficient botheration,
(When moon and stars were clouded, and no illumination
Appeared in neighbouring cottages to afford an intimation
To the luckless traveller) without this infernal excavation.

For these and other reasons, then, of which the enumeration
Would swell to inconvenience the Secretary's communication,
The Colonists' Society would be glad of information
As to what's intended to be done about the restoration
Of the Market-place at Christchurch to its original elevation.

September, 1852.

The Shagroon's Lament. [4)

"The climate of New Zealand is superior to the south of France."—Extract from a Canterbury Settler's Letter.

AMONG the dreary mountains, far up above the gorge,
There lives a potent demon, ever working at his forge;
A worker at the winds is he, a flatulent old buffer,
And he sends his manufactures down that man and beast may suffer.

I've witnessed all the winds that blow, from Land's End to Barbadoes—
Typhoons, pamperos, hurricanes, eke terrible tornadoes.
All these but gentle zephyrs are, which pleasantly go by ye,
To the howling, bellowing, horrid gusts which sweep down the Rakaia.

That little cloud now sailing down is foreman at the bellows.
At Mount Hutt's base he'll take his place to overlook his fellows;
There's Gust and Puff, and Shriek and Howl, and demons without number;
And they're coming now, with dusky brow, to waken summer's slumber.

They're armed with the winds of the wild west coast,
  Which they've cooled in the mountain snow;
And they're riding down on their steeds of dust,
  Making dismal havoc below.

The crops which looked bright in the summer's light,
  And pleasantly waved in the breeze,
Are wither'd and dead, the unripe grain shed,
  And leafless the rocking trees.

All huddled in vain are the sheep on the plain,
  Destruction is nearing them fast;
And the cry of the lamb, as it bleats to its dam,
  Is mingling its tones with the blast.

And the settler at morn may well look forlorn,
  As he hastens in search of his flock;
For lambs dead or dying, and ewes fled or flying,
  His hopes of prosperity mock.

The Prince of the Air is roused from his lair,
  And howls in his bullying might;
The gravel and dust are now mixed with the gust,
  And the demons shriek out with delight.

The wild pigs sniff the air, and with grunts they declare
  They'll be hanged if they stand such a gale;
While both barrows and boars, and sows by the scores
  Cut their sticks with the wind at their tail.

The garden—my joy—my leisure's employ!—
  Where are now thy flowers or thy trees?
They are blackened and bruised and most awfully used,
  With the cabbages, carrots, and peas.

The onions are whipp'd, the potatoes are nipp'd,
  The willows have lost every leaf;
The fruit trees are dead, or torn from their bed,
  And the gardener is dying of grief.

Oh! Squatters, beware of the Powers of the Air,
When you come with your cattle or sheep;
For New Zealand's a spot just loosed out of pot,
And the wind there is never asleep.

It comes from the South with a burst in its mouth,
Bringing snow, sleet, or drizzling rain;
Or it changes to West, and does its behest,
With a blast twice as furious again.

The vessels at sea stout and strong tho' they be,
Are totally lost to command;
Their canvas is rent, their strong masts are bent,
Or they're hopelessly cast on the strand.

The best of good fellows can't stand the strong bellows,
That are ever at work on this shore;
So stick where you are, it is better by far,
Than come here and be heard of no more.

M. P. S.

May, 1852.

The Overseer's Lament. (5)

Adopted from Hood's "Song of the Shirt," to the circumstances of an Overseer in the service of Long Clarke.

WITH breeches thread-bare and worn,
With jumper running to seed,
An overseer sat in a stringy-bark hut,
Smoking his favourite weed.
Puff! puff! puff!
"Oh! when shall I rise from this state?"
And still with a voice of dolorous pitch
He sang the song of his fate.

"Ride! ride! ride!
While the cock is crowing aloof!
And ride—ride—ride;
Till the stars shine thro' the roof!
It's oh, to be a Super
Along with some western swell,
Where man has never a stiver to save,
But sometimes gets a spell.

"Ride! ride! ride!
Till my boots are rusty and worn!
And ride—ride—ride!
Till my breeches are tattered and torn;
Plain, and gully, and range,
Range, and gully, and plain,
Till over the saddle I fall asleep,
To waken and ride again.

"Oh! Squatters with beautiful runs!
Oh! Squatters with fattening plains!
Not feed alone are you wearing out,
But you're sowing rheumatic pains!
Twitch! twitch! twitch!
I feel it in all my bones,
Sowing at once with a double stitch,
Colonial experience and groans.

"But why do I talk of rheumatics?
That phantom of aching bone,
I hardly fear his terrible shape,
It seems so like my own—
It seems so like my own,
Because of the spills I reap.*
Oh! that runs should be so dear,
And overseers so cheap!

---

* Clarke's horses are notorious buck-jumpers.

"Ride! ride! ride!
My labour never flags;
And what are its wages? Forty a year,
And these two wretched nags.
This mutton-chop – and this damper queer—
A stretcher—a 'possum rug—
And so, wretched all that the traveller here
But seldom shows his mug!

"Count! count! count!
The thousands of every flock.
Count—count—count!
Till I've counted my master's stock;
Ewes, and wethers, and lambs
Lambs, and wethers, and ewes,
Till the eyes are dazzled, the hurdles smashed,
And my shins are all in a bruise.

"Snip! snip! snip!
When the shearing season's come,
And snip—snip—snip!
But never a keg of rum!
Curse, and squabble, and row,
Row, and squabble, and curse,
Till my eyes are blackened, my 'claret' drawn,
As well as my private purse.

"Oh but to breathe the breath
Of the Royal Hotel in town;
A prime Manilla in my mouth,
Whilst I knock my earnings down!
Oh! but for one short month,
To spree as I used to spree,
Before I knew the Super's berth,
In the days when I was free!

"Oh, but for one short week!
A respite, however brief!
No blessed leisure for love or lush,
But only time for grief!
A little drinking would ease my mind,
But in its secret lurk
The grog must stop, for every drop
Would hinder station work!"

With breeches thread-bare and worn,
With jumper running to seed,
An overseer sat in a stringy-bark hut,
Smoking his favourite weed.
Puff! puff! puff!
Oh when shall I rise from this state?
And still with a tone like a heart-broken lark—
Would that its wail would reach Long Clarke—
He sang the song of his fate.

M, P. S.

January, 1853.

The Lay of the last Registered Dog. ([6])

TEN BOB to his friends, dogs, horses, and men,
Sends growling, and takes up his very best pen
To describe how his health has been falling away
Since these horrid elections have carried the sway,
Before any writs had arrived from the North,
I could rise every morning and freely go forth,
Without smile from the vicar, or snarl from the mob,
Like a free, independent, and easy Ten Bob:
But no sooner had Governor Greyhound's despatch
Appointed the days for each course of the match,
Than all former connexions were thrown to the wind;
No two dogs in the country could bark in one mind;

No dog knew his master, no man knew his dog,
And our puppies were lost in political fog!
The Superintendent's election came first;
Some thought one dog best, and some thought him the worst;
But at length it was left to three claimants alone
To fight for the Government collar and bone.
The first was a dog of undoubted renown,
Who had long kept a watch in our waterside town;
By the name on his collar his sires had seen
Many fights with the wild wolves in Ireland green.
The second, a bloodhound of Norman descent,
Whose forefathers once to the Holy Land went;
And 'tis thought in his heart a good portion there lurks
Of the courage his ancestors show'd to the Turks.
The third, a Scotch terrier, stricken in years;
"Who" some saucy dog screamed in my wondering ears,
"Though often in battle, yet never was wounded,
"And still is alive although once he was drowned!"
Now the two first went off, much like weasels asleep,
In the desert to watch over cattle and sheep;
And the terrier came forward, as wise as an owl,
And his mongrel assembly raised up a loud howl:
"See how bravely our dog wears his ribbons and collars;
"See what very nice bones for each bully that follows!
"Cheap kennels! cheap bones! of short commons no danger
"All dogs, if they please, shall be dogs-in-the-manger!
"Those other two hounds do not merit your bark;
"They are seeking to give you a bite in the dark;
"And to mock you by sending for *men* who wear tails,
"Who *curtail* in small shoes their young ladies' toenails,
"Can't say 'bow-wow' in English, eat rice grown in bogs,
"Which they flavour with birds' nests and fat little dogs!
"If they sent for a troop of industrious fleas,
"'Twere not half such a curse as the horrid Chinese!"
Away stayed the bloodhound, and back came the watch-dog.
But almost too late to outflank the old Scotch dog;

Till at length the poor terrier was fairly outbid,
When his foe snubbed Celestials as other dogs did,
Then we underwent flattery, threats and defiance,
Unfriendly disruption, unholy alliance,
Nonsensical claptrap, in sounding orations,
And unconstitutional Associations.
Every wretched dog's life was a dog's life indeed ;
For, whether of spaniel or pig-hunting breed,
He was sure to be fawned on or barked at all day ;
The cupboard was bare if he voted one way,
Since his master had threatened to give him the sack ;
If he didn't he'd cold shoulder get from the pack ;
How to judge, though for judgment a regular Daniel,
Whether best one should vote with the bull-dog or spaniel ?
We changed our opinions and changed them again,
As much like vain dogs as a vessel's dog-vane.
How it ended I really don't know and don't care,
For I soon got as cross as a sore-headed bear ;
And I grumble whenever I hear the bare name
Of the head of the poll or electoral claim.
I assure all my friends it's my dogged desire
All placards and addresses were stuffed in the fire ;
And I vote that some Governor, Beadle, or King,
Be appointed at once to dissolve the whole thing !

* * * * * * *

Well, they tell me that not such bad dogs after all,
Have been chosen for each empty kennel and stall ;
My humour and health both begin to feel better,
So I'll just give the members, to finish my letter,
Advice which one candidate boldly defied,
(Although Wellington's own, as the very best guide
To a youthful M.P. for the house that he sate in)—
"Know your mind ! Mind you speak it ! and never quote Latin !"

E. J. W.

September, 1853.

Proclamation

ON THE COSTUMES AND CUSTOMS OF NEW ZEALAND.

WHEREAS I, the Governor, still have the right
To make laws, and give orders for every known thing;
And Acts are mere cobwebs while mine is the might!
Now this is the will of your Deputy-King!

The Treasurers all shall be dressed in dark *grey*,
With a leech on the collar, and a sponge on the wrist;
And a gold-digger's jumper to wear on pay-day,
Bedizened all over with strong silver twist.

All Crown Land Commissioners henceforth shall wear
A *rouge-et-noir* coat, with dice for the buttons;
At a thimble-rig table from Bartlemy fair
Distributing runs to good owners of muttons.

Their Surveyors, jackets of fanciful hue,
Very loose, and cut out of a pretty sketch-map;
Their tools and their boots shall be shining and new;
They shall sit on a stool, near a peg for their cap.

Representative men shall wear night-caps of wool,
And warm flannel jackets like players at cricket,
For fear their ambition should sicken and cool,
While they fag all around me and I keep the wicket.

And if they turn rusty with nothing to do,
Since I put off their innings beyond next December,
They may play out their honours at whist or at loo;
For while I am the belly who cares for a member?

The life-nominees shall wear long-faced bell-toppers,
And plumes of white feathers to hide their disgrace;
Their coats shall be turned, and their pockets be woppers,
To hold solid smiles from my Majesty's face.

I myself wear chain-mail, as a sign of my reign,
The bold leader and chief of this glittering band;
And the King of six Provinces still shall obtain
His throne from dear rule, and his *crowns* from cheap land.

September, 1853. E. J. W

Canterbury in September, 1853.

AS when a stream, long chafing to be free
From narrowing banks that do its course restrain,
From rocky islet's intercepting chain,
And tangled over-growth and drifting tree,
Forth bursts at length from dull obscurity,
And sweeps majestic through a boundless plain;
So have I seen an infant State remain
Long trammel'd by obstructive policy,
Misgovernment, official prejudice;
Numb'd by suspense, and chill'd by mystery.
At length free scope is giv'n. I see it rise
Strong, active, self-reliant. May we see,
Who watch thy course with loving, anxious eyes,
Thy promise ripen to maturity!

J.

September, 1853.

"Greece is, where the Greeks are."

"'TIS Greece, where Greeks do dwell!" So spake and [thought
That ancient race. The isle-embroidered sea
Was sprinkled with their towns; lo! spreading free
One Greece in many lands. May we be taught
By them to love our country as we ought!
'Tis not thy soil, O England! nor thy scenes,
Though oft on these home-wand'ring Fancy leans;
'Tis not alone th' historic fervour caught
From old association; not thy marts,
Nor e'en thy grey cathedrals, nor thy wells
Of ancient learning, though for these our hearts
May fondly yearn; true love of country tells
A better tale—thy Church, thy laws, thy arts!
'Tis England where an English spirit dwells.

J.

November, 1853.

The Avon.

"Fies nobilium tu quoque fontium."—Hor.

I LOVE thee, Avon! though thy banks have known
No deed of note, thy wand'ring course along
No bard of Avon hath pour'd forth in song
Thy tuneful praise; thy modest tide hath flown
For centuries on, unheeded and alone.
I love thee for thy English name, but more
Because my countrymen along thy shore
Have made new homes. Therefore not all unknown
Henceforth thy streams shall flow. A little while
Shall see thy wastes grow lovely. Not in vain
Shall England's sons dwell by thee many a mile.
With verdant meads and fields of waving grain
Thy rough uncultur'd banks ere long shall smile;
Heav'n-pointing spires shall beautify thy plain.

J.

January, 1854.

An Historical Picture.

BEHOLD, O England! from thy sea-girt throne
The daughter-nations gath'ring to thy feet;
From East and West, from North and South they meet,
Those thou hast rear'd, and claimest for thine own;
Bid them draw near, survey them one by one;—
See, last of all before thee trembling stoop
The youngest daughter of the circling group.
By filial look and close resemblance known—
She kneels before thee and thy blessing seeks!
Heir of thy glorious past, she craves to be
Heir of thy virtues, all that Hist'ry speaks
Of brave, large-hearted, noble, wise in thee,
Thy Truth, thy Justice, and that Light which streaks
Thy foulest page, thy native Piety,

J.

April, 1854.

The Battle of Sinope

"Assyrios complexa sinus stat *Opima* Sinope."—VAL. FLACC.

WELLNIGH two thousand years have sped their flight
Since the proud Roman trod beneath his feet
Thy wealth, Sinope! thy sea bord'ring street,
Strew'd with barbaric spoil, confess'd the might
Of the world's victors. Still untamed in fight,
The Pontic hero all undaunted stood,
A rock unmov'd amidst a whelming flood.
Once more Sinope mourns a tearful sight;
The Northern Eagle swoops, his wrath to wreak
In savage fury on his helpless prey.
God help thee, England, to defend the weak!
Who groan beneath Oppression's scorching ray
Thy island-covert shall not vainly seek;
The Tyrant shall not prosper in his day.

J.

May, 1854.

[NOTE.—Sinope, the scene of the late sea-fight, if it may be so called, between the Russians and the Turks, fills a page in ancient history, having been taken by the Roman general Lucullus, in the war with Mithridates, the heroic King of Pontus, the most obstinate of all the antagonists of Rome. It was taken in the year 71 B.C. Sinope is also famous as the birth-place of Diogenes the Cynic. It is singular that it should have retained its ancient name to the present day, when it has become the theatre of an event more remarkable in itself, and more important in its consequences.]

Tobacco.

UPON his mouth may curses fall;
May it be dead to savour;
His mellow fruits be cinders dry,
His wines devoid of flavour;
His bread be sawdust in his jaws,
And may his teeth so black, oh,
Turn all his sweets to bitter sour—
The wretch who chews tobacco!

Upon his nose may curses light;
  May odours never charm it;
May garden flowers and woods and bowers
  Yield noxious scents to harm it;
May all Arabia's spice exhale
  Foul gas to make it suffer,
Who makes a dusthole of his mouth—
  The vile tobacco-snuffer!

May never lady press his lips,
  His proffered love returning,
Who makes a furnace of his mouth,
  And keeps its chimney burning!
May each true woman shun his sight,
  For fear his fumes might choke her;
And none but hags, who smoke themselves,
  Have kisses for a smoker!

February, 1855.

Charades on Unpopular Subjects. (7)

No. 1.

"*Here we go up, up, up.*"

THE morning is all sunshine,
  The bridal guests are met;
But the Father frets, the Mother fumes,
  For the bridegroom comes not yet.
He's here, and from the saddle
  With joyous haste he springs,
And on his charger's glossy neck
  My first impatient flings.

The bonds that ne'er are broken
  Have joined those twain in one;
The words of blessing spoken—
  And from the church they're gone.

Oh! blest in youth, and hope, and love,
May years fleet by as hours;
And all good Powers unite to strew
Your *second* with life's flowers!

The mother gazes after
With tears she fain would hide,
As lessening in her straining sight
Those two beloved ones ride.
I hear a plunge, a scream, a fall—
And vain is human aid;
Among the pitfalls of my *whole*
That bride is lowly laid.

ANSWER.

And pray what may the riddle mean?
I pray, kind reader, tell.
It hath an answer dark, I ween,
And deep as hidden well.
What is it makes the cross more cross,
And stirs the meek to wrath?
What but the holes, and pits, and ruts
That stud our *Bridle Path*.

S. R.

August, 1856.

No. 2.

"An old tale, and often told."

SIR Hugh he had passed a restless night—
He woke at the earliest touch of light,
One fair and frosty morning;
The sun was rising—all earth seemed gay;
And *my first*, bedecking each blade and spray,
Shone bright in the glorious dawning;

"My life," quoth he, "is very slow,
I'm weary of sheep, and smoke, and sighs,
The sky is as blue as Ellen's eyes,
The road and its dangers I'll despise,
And to Christchurch I will go."

Merrily on through flax and sand,
Merrily over the fern-grown land,
He rode with a loosened rein!
Firmly and fleetly his charger trode
As he neared his lady love's abode;
And nor care nor stay did his heart forbode,
Till he came to where a Government road
Traversèd the swampy plain;
A moment he paused, for he oft had heard
How that road grew worse the more it was stirred,
And with damage and danger was strowed;
But he thought of his coat so spick and span,
And the boots he had blacked with his "ain richt han',"
And he looked at the swamp—unhappy man!
And onward, alas! he rode.
Perchance had he known that a week before
That luckless road was "mended,"
The doubts with which his mind ran o'er
Far otherwise had ended.

But nothing knew he—that wight so green—
How manuka branches, (*) with holes between,
Far down in the mud had plunged been,
A pitfall for man and beast I ween!
So on he rode towards fair Ellen's home,
And on welcome kind he reckoned,—
When his horse gave one plunge and then stood still,
In despair to achieve *my second*.

No more do I know; whether out he came;
Or on what, or whom they laid the blame

Of rider in tatters, and steed dead lame,
From Ellen and oats debarred!
I know but that, while in the mud so soft
He bewailed his fate so hard,
My whole came by on a dray aloft,
And indited this charade.

S. R.

September, 1856.

No. 3.

"Leave that wreath to wither upon the cold bank there."
T. H. BAYLEY.

WITH eager speed along the plain
A youth and maiden ride;
Fondly on her his gaze is bent
Unheeding aught beside.
Unseen, far down the glorious west,
The summer sunset glows;
Unnoted, to the evening breeze
My *first* its fragance throws.

He speaks at length—And art thou then
Mine own for grief and glee;
And wilt thou never once regret
The wealth thou leav'st for me?
My *second* is a lowly home
For one so fair as thou;
But love shall smooth thy path, and chase
Each furrow from thy brow.

They near my *whole*—that barrier past,
Pursuit they may defy;
Oh, joy! to see its waters gleam
Beneath the star-lit sky.

Why weeps the bride, her perils o'er?
  Whence comes that boding sigh?
Alas! upon the further shore
  The punt lies high and dry!

MORAL.

ADDRESSED TO PARENTS AND GUARDIANS.

'Tis true, you may say,
That for once in a way
  The Ferryman's care was all right.
For a run-away pair,
Whether here or elsewhere,
  Deserve to be stopped in their flight.

But remember, I pray,
In this fabulous lay
  I have dwelt but on what *might* accrue;
While the plague and the loss,
We all know to our cost,
  Are both real, important, and true.

The butcher, the baker,
The candlestick maker,
  All find it detestable, very;
For their mutton grows bad,
And their bread becomes sad,
  While they wait at the *Heathcote* Ferry.

S. R.

September, 1856.

No. 4.

"It's as true as taxes is—and nothing's truer than them."

THE sky is bright, the breeze is fair;
  With mainsail flowing free
And lifelike grace, a gallant bark
Is bounding o'er the sea.

What seeks *my first* across that azure deep?
Would he his soul in dreams of beauty steep
'Mid the green isles of glittering tropic seas?
Or is his pennon waving in the breeze
To prove that England's lion does not sleep,
But over English homes a watch doth keep,
Guarding her hearths ev'n in the hour of peace?
Oh! no! he seeks a distant shore
With heart intent on gold;
A long percentage in his head,
And blue shirts in his hold!

They near the coasts of sunny France,
My second to descry:
An islet crowned by one dark mass
Of frowning masonry.*
And many a tale the captain tells
Of captives in its gloomy cells
Shut from the light of day;
Prisoners untried—their guilt unproved,
Torn from their homes and all they loved,
To pine their lives away.
The port is gained—no buyers come;
He speaks, his venture ruing,
"Can this be busy Lyttelton?
What are the Customs doing? (⁹)
Why don't they 'clear' my shirts so blue,
So fit for every station?"
Alack! two thousand cocoa-nuts
Have found them occupation!
With yard-wands stretched and brows perplexed,
They seek their cubic measure,
To "square the circle" striving still
In most profound displeasure.

---

* A nautical reader may suggest the grave practical inconvenience of making the Chateau d'If on a voyage from Gravesend to Lyttelton. That was the Captain's affair.

And "Cease," they cry, "to tempt our view
With fustian strong and serge of blue
  We cannot—dare not—buy:
My whole ordains that by their weight,
And not their worth, unto the State
  All things their tribute pay;
And we, concealing all our ire,
On light things fixing our desire,
Must learn to 'walk in silk attire'
  From pure economy."

S. R.

September, 1856.

No. 5.

"Pitch thy behaviour low, thy projects high."—G HERBERT.

WE left our homes with hearts elate,
  Utopian visions dreaming;
"Adieu," we cried, "to tax and rate,
Adieu to wrangling and debate,
Adieu to strife 'twixt Church and State,
  And welcome hope and freedom!"
As brothers all we meant to live,
To age, and birth, and wisdom give
  The honour each beseeming;
And feed our woolly flocks in peace,
Till they grew betimes to a golden fleece,
  On Union Banks bright gleaming!
Alas! alack! the space how far
'Twixt things that seem and things that are,
  Stern truth and the mind's bright phantom!
Our beautiful church is tumbling down, (10)
And over its relics we fight and frown,
  In a manner far from handsome;
While the road that we planned from town to town,
(At the cost of three miles for ten thousand poun');
May be done—if between whiles we're not done brown—
  In the time of our son's son's grandson.

And for fleece of gold—(Oh! prince of flams)!
Sure ne'er, since the time of Cromwell's Lambs,
Were sheep so contumacious;
They won't stay at home—they won't be shorn—
To plague out our lives they were surely born,
Their ways are so audacious!
They're always to seek when guests are met,
And mutton is wanted, or weather is wet;
And, last and worst, the scab they get,
And we're fined by Inspectors grim;
And poor "Fair Play" is called hard names,
Because he objects to various games
Which don't play fair by him!
In short, the thing I'm doing now,
And which you, who read with bended brow,
Are going to do at me,
My first, which we do *sans* pause or rest,
Is the thing of things which we do the best
In this pattern colony.

And yet I see the time will come
When this, our new and distant home,
Shall be glorious, great, and free;
Great in the glory of mighty sons,
Free with the one true freedom,
(The liberty demagogues never know,
Alas—that our voters heed 'em!)
The freedom which gives and will ever show
Respect for the good and great below;
Nor—though its own talents be but so-so—
Deems (like them) each wiser man its foe.
I know that the day shall dawn at last,
When, petty strifes and cavils past,
We all shall work together;
When New Zealand's swamps shall laugh with corn.
In her joyous summer weather;
When we travellers, not as now forlorn,
In fear to lose *my second*,

Shall be borne on *my whole* across her plains,
With wheels for a charger, and steam for reins,
Wherever a wish has beckoned;
When the hateful "nobbler" shall be forgot,
(That snare to our voters "scot and lot,")
And we smoke our pipes o'er a cheerful pot
Of home-brewed ale, blithe humming!
So reader kind, unbend your brow,
And let me make my parting bow
To the tune of "A good time coming."

S. R.

November, 1856.

No. 6.

"Look on this picture, and on this."

I SLEPT—and back to England's shore
My gladsome fancy roved;
And my free feet trod her daisied sod
'Mid the scenes and the friends I loved;
And I marvelled much at each proof of might,
For, so long unseen, each common sight—
Each road, and carriage, and gas-lamp bright—
Was a wonder fresh for me.
But the marvel that left me dumb-foundered quite
Was a genuine May Fair Exquisite,
With his shiny boots, and his hand so white,
And his wondrous self-elation;
And his coat, (oh! garment of little ease!),
So guiltless of wrinkle, line, or crease:
That he might have been from nose to knees
Done up in boards—like a bungling piece
Of Colonial legislation!
In sooth, this Knight of ladies gay,
This kind of carpet Bayard,
Was scented and curled in such a way
That at sight of him my thoughts would stray

Far back to Assyria's palmy day,
And *my first*, as described in Tennyson's lay,
Or "imported neat" by Layard.

Once more I dreamed, and now again
I stood on our Canterbury Plain;—
He stood beside me there.
But oh! how changed; where that bright vest?
That faultless coat and padded chest?
Sad echo answers "Where?"
Gone is his hat so tall and trim;
A wide-awake with half a brim
Conceals *my second* now;
As broken in fortune, but stout of limb,
(For misfortune has made a man of him!)
He drives *my whole* his bread to win,
Or sometimes speeds the plough.
And "Oh," he cries, "that our Government roads
"Were like our Government laws!
"For in *them* you can drive your coach and six
"With ease through every clause;
"While in *these* my dray with its team of ten
"Is doomed to stick and pause;
"Till I wish our Councillors wise were here
"To enjoy the mess they cause;
"No help would I give but a loud *Hear! hear!*
"And '*laughter*' and '*much applause*.'"

S. R.

December, 1856.

No. 7.

"Oh! dear! how shall I marry me?
Oh! dear! how shall I woo?"

WITHIN a stately English home
A maiden fair I see;
"She is bright and young, and her glory comes
Of an ancient ancestry!"

Gentle and graceful and beautiful,
  In wealth and luxury nurst,
Her every gesture, look, and tone,
  Bespeak *my* highborn *first*.

Before her bends a form I know,
  Though he is greatly changed
Since from his far New Zealand home
  His wandering steps have ranged;
For he is drest in Stultz's best,
  As you may plainly see,
And, instead of fustian, broad-cloth fine
  Arrays his bended knee.

But the face is the same, and 'tis one I ween
  A maiden may love to see,
With its bright dark eye and chestnut curls
  And smile so frank and free;
Then why doth my first contract her brow
  As thus he tells *my second;*
As she would say—"Sir guest, I trow,
If you thought in me to find a "vrow"
  Without your host you reckoned."

"Oh dearest, fairest, best of all,
  Say, wilt thou fly with me
Across two oceans' silvery foam,
  My bride and my pride to be?
I know that your voice is clear and sweet
  As the swan's last fabled lay,
And your step in the dance as light and fleet
  As Ellsler or Duvernay.
I know you can draw with ease and skill
  Men, cattle, flowers, and fences,
And 'bosky bourne' and pebbly rill,
  And likewise—inferences.

But can you 'call the cattle home,'
  And dance the dance they'll lead you?
And can your skill 'fine-draw' my coat
  If rents perchance should need you?
Oh, can you china leave for delf?
  Or—what I own is harder—
Say, can you 'lady's maid' yourself?
And, while you *hook* your dress behind,
Still keep an *eye* before, and mind
    The pantry and the larder?

"And can you roast, and boil, and bake,
And dainty bread with soda make?
  For, though I myself don't pamper,
Still if, whene'er the yeast turns sour,
Your bonny brow begins to lower,
  My *Fair* will prove a *damper*.
But, if these trifles you can learn,
Likewise to starch, and iron, and churn,
  Nor fear to cross the sea!
Then, dearest, fairest, best of all,
  Then mays't thou fly with me,
And reign my Queen in kitchen and hall,
  My *whole* for aye to be!"

S. R.

December, 1856.

No. 8.

"While sages prate and courts debate
  The same stars set and shine;
And the world as it rolled through Twenty Eight
  Will roll through Twenty Nine."—Praed.

THE Council is summoned, the Speaker is there,
  And our law-givers wise are met
With potent, grave, and reverend air,
  In expectation set.

Oh! had I the brush of a Douw or Vandyke,
Of Lawrence, or Phillips, or even Van Eyck,
(He who paints his old ladies so nice and so like,)
Or a cast-off pen of Macaulay—
I might show how they look'd, and what they said;
How the wise ones dosed or the paper read;
And the busy ones came alway,
Each armed with a mighty paper scroll,
(*My first*) done up in portentous roll,
Containing his private project fine
For the cure of every want and crime,
Each social need of the place and time
One by means of a tramway line
From everywhere to nowhere;
And one for suppressing drunkenness,
Enacting—to save all labour—
That whenever a colonist takes too much
We should straightway fine his neighbour.
In short, so much of *my first* was there,
That our profoundest thinkers
Seemed to me, (Oh, pardon this idle rhyme!)
Like twopenny postmen at Christmas time,
Or some new sort of Ornithorhynchus.
But now the time will soon be here
When, no longer fancy free,
But sorry at heart and sick at head,
Bumping about on a villainous bed
Till *my second* they'll surely be,
The chosen few o'er *my whole* shall steer,
From Lyttelton jetty to Manakau pier,
In the famous "Zingari;"
Where I hope, though I scarcely dare to think,
(For I can't quite all probabilities blink)
They won't make such a mess of their statesmanship;
That they may be glad at home to stay
In peace and quiet for many a day,
From the cares of office free. S. R.

December, 1856.

A Lay of the Sumner Road. (11)

"The first person of rank who is killed will put everything in order."—SYDNEY SMITH's letters on Railways.

I.

IT was a goodly muster
  Upon a Monday morn,
When the Council in a cluster
  Went to view that road forlorn.
On Sunday night each quaking man
Had gather'd round him all his clan,
A long, a last farewell had said,
And then despairing went to bed.

II.

But the thought came with the morrow,—
  Is this our valour's worth?
Shall our hearts be sunk in sorrow
  When our country calls us forth?
We'll brave the point of Moabone;
And, reckless of each falling stone,
Each quivering bog, each dizzie crag,
Boldly we'll march on legs or nag.

III.

The valiant vow is utter'd;
  The gallant deed is done;
Though many a bosom flutter'd
  The Ferry Punt is won.
Of all that noble Council train
Not one is in a quagmire slain!
Not one is carrion on the wild!
Not one is lost to wife or child!

IV.

Oh! on that famous morning,
  Had but one member died!
None could have missed the warning
  Which from his body hied:—
"The road is doom'd." But now, alas!
We must go round by Evans' pass,
Because no hero, all on fire,
Like Marcus Curtius, would expire.

V.

What! is there no "bravo Roland,
  The flower of chivalry?"
Not one in all this slow land
  Who'll die to set us free?
Methinks I hear a whisp'ring sigh—
'Oh! no, we *never will say die!*'
Ah! treach'rous boast! ye recreant ten!
Say die for once, and die like men.

VI.

Go, Patriots, call a quorum,
  And be this your battle cry:—
"Est dulce et decorum
  Pro Bridle-path mori!"
Meet! spout! divide, and pick your man!
Send him to glory while you can!
And this shall be his requiem grim,
"We smash'd the road, for it smashed him."

G. C.

December, 1856.

Provincial Parodies.

No. 1.
RAILROADIOR. (12)

PROVINCIAL funds were falling fast,
When to the Council Chamber passed
A man who held, in red tape tied,
A paper with this word outside—
"Railroadior!"

His mouth half grinned; his eye, with a wink,
Flashed like a blot of bright red ink;
And, like a song by Grisi sung,
This word flowed from his well-oiled tongue—
"Railroadior!"

In members' eyes he saw the doubt,
The objection to his scheme peep out.
Within, THE GRAND IDEA shone,
And he replied, still pressing on,—
"Railroadior!"

"Try not the tramway," old hands said,
"Loose hang the boulders over head;
The work is long, and the cost is high;"
"Hang the expense" was his reply;
"Railroadior!"

"Oh! stay thee," Christchurch cried, "and spend
Thy surplus cash upon this end!"
A mental thumb went to his nose,
In mute reply this word he shows—
"Railroadior!"

"Beware the road along the tide!
Beware the hole in the hill's inside!"
This was the public's parting prayer.
A voice said, with an off-hand air—
"Railroadior!"

As, at the end of many a year,
The then Provincial Engineer
Surveyed the long-projected track,
A sheet blew by, with printed back,—
"Railroadior!"

A tramway, where the new road wound,
Half buried in the soil was found!
And on a stick, with red tape tied,
A paper with this word outside,—
"Railroadior!"

There, in the midst of rocks and clay,
Useless but wonderful it lay;
And scornful voices echoed far,
From Christchurch to the Sumner bar,—
"Railroadior!"

C. W.

October, 1856.

No. 2.
THE STRUGGLE OF PAPANUI.

AT Christchurch, at the dawn of day,
All mudless stood the unloaded dray;
And in the stockyard, near it, lay
Eight bullocks, waiting patiently.

The driver thought it not so nice
That afternoon, when clocks struck twice,
Plunging in swamps and mud-stained ice,
The deepness of the axle-tree.

In slush and quagmire 'fast as nails'
The oxen lash their muddy tails;
But furious still the driver flails,
And double-thongs unceasingly.

Then plunge the steers to anger driven,
Then snaps the pole with plunges riven,
And, louder than these noises even,
Sharp cracks the whipcord stingingly.

But heavier yet that whip must drop
On mud-stuck oxen, neck and crop;
And longer yet that dray must stop,
Imbedded to its axle-tree.

'Tis road. But scarce the stoutest one
Can ford the mud-lake rolling dun;
Where artful drains that wrong-way run
Pour down their waters constantly!

The quagmire thickens; on ye pack!
Through slimy swamps and spongy track.
Crack, driver, all thy whipcord crack!
And shout with all thy ribaldry!

Few, few will cart, such holes to meet!
Each swamp will lower the price of wheat;
And every road be called a feat
Of Government perversity.

C. W.

November, 1856.

No. 3.

ROAD LINES. ([13])

BELIEVE me, if all those tremendous big holes,
Which I view on thy causeway to-day,
Were to-morrow bridged over with scrub and with poles,
And craftily covered with clay,
Thou would'st still be no use, as this moment thou art,
Let the Government say as they will,
For thy precious zig-zags are too steep for a cart,
And we're hopeless of holes in thy hill.

C. W.

November, 1856.

No. 4.

THE TOWN OF CHRISTCHURCH. ([14])

AIR.—"Groves of Blarney."

OH! the Town of Christchurch
Is an elegant mixture
Of roads and pasture
And swamp and sand;
So widely stretching
In each direction,
From Brittan's section
To Caulfield's land.

Oh! fifty twenties
The whole extent is
Of English acres,
All in a square:
And plenty of space is
In the vacant places,
With patches of praties
Lying here and there.

Oh! when you enter
You're in the centre
Of houses in plenty
    On every hand;
There's more than twenty,
Both full and empty,
And the Superintendent's
    Is very grand.

And there's public houses,
Where whoever chooses
Walks in and carouses
    On the best of fare;
But the distant Royal
Is, without denial,
The biggest of all,
    Beyond compare.

And there's many a mansion
Of grand expansion;
And some I could mention,
    That could'nt be beat;
And there's tidy villas
With weeping willows,
And one with pillars
    In Cashel Street.

Oh! that's the location
That's the admiration
Of the population
    Both far and wide;
For in two rows neatly,
All down the street, the
Houses stand in it,
    On every side.

And there's loud resounding
From the iron foundry ;
And the Union Bank
    Has an office there;
And there's Mister Packer,
And there once was Thacker ;
But Doctor Barker
    Is in Cathedral Square.

Now them that governs
This noble province
Has a gorgeous office
    That you'll quite admire ;
But the way into the building
Is most bewildering,
So the officials and children
    Slip through the wires ;

And there there's verandahs
Above two of the windows ;
But the other end is
    Eutirely bare;
And there's a big sun-dial
Stuck up for a trial
How long the sky 'll
    Continue fair.

Now the rooms are spacious
And multifarious ;
The chief secretary is
    Under the tiles;
But the elegant chamber
Of the legislature
Is the grandest feature
    Of this noble pile.

And a new and grand set
Stands over against it,
(Though theyr'e not commenced yet,)
On the other side
Of the river Avon,
That through flax leaves waving
Is the water-cresses laving
With her silver tide.

But long is the narration
Of the situation,
Which my poor genius
Can not entwine:
But were I the writer
Of the Christchurch paper,
'Tis in every feature
I would make it shine.

C. W.

December, 1857.

No. 5.

BALLAD OF THE ANCIENT MEMBER. (15)

"Quorum pars magua fui."

AIR—"Ben Bolt."

OH! don't you remember FitzGerald, my boy?
FitzGerald who used so to teaze;
Who soaped us all down when we ventured to frown,
And frown'd when we most wish'd to please.
The wind blows fresh on FitzGerald, my boy,
As he ploughs through the salt sea foam;
Oh! I'd like to ship for the same sort of trip,
And be paid, my old boy, to go home!

Oh! don't you remember the chamber, my boy,
Our first Parliamentary Shop?
With the skylights above, and the four bare walls,
And the rain pouring in from the top.
There Bills we could quietly pass, my boy;
And Bills we could quietly shelve:
But now we've to mix among twenty and six,
Instead of the olden twelve.

And don't you remember J.B———n, my boy,
The eloquent Secreta-ry?
Who managed things here after turning you out,
And was then tumbled over* by me.
In the country far distant from town, my boy,
All desolate, drear, and alone,
Some people exist among tussocks and sheep;
And B———n looks after his own.

And don't you remember our stormy debates?
And the nice indiscriminate way
In which bitter antagonists over-night
Would vote side by side the next day?
There were numbers who sat on the Government seats
In the jolly days gone by;
But of all the men who were ministers then
There remain but you and I.

And don't you remember old S—w—l, my boy?
And C——s, smiling gaily at care;
And H—m—lt—n, the spark, and A—lm—r, the clerk,
And S—m—n, the first in the chair.
There's a change in the men that we talk to, my boy;
There's a change which may make us look blue,
But I don't think you see any changes in me:
And I see no change in you.

C. W.

January, 1858.

* This is rather too strong an expression for the fact.

No. 6.

SONG OF THE SQUATTERS. ([16])

AFTER LONGFELLOW

WOULD you hear a pretty story
Of our ancient legislators,
Of our statesmen in the old time,
Of the councillors and wise men
In the very ancient ages?
Shall I tell you how the stockmen,
Crafty squatters, subtle shepherds,
From the Southward and the Northward,
From the deep and wide Waitangi,
From the changing Hurunui,
From the gloomy Harewood forest,
From the icy lake of Coleridge,
From the country of Mackenzie,
From the regions of the Westward,
Came together down to Christchurch,
Entered the Provincial Council,
Made orations in the Council,
Begged, implored, and prayed the Council,
Coaxed the unsuspecting Council;
Hoaxed the simple-minded Council,
Did the very wily statesmen,
Gammoned all the legislators,
Humbugged, diddled, all the members,
And departed, laughing, chuckling,
With their thumbs up to their noses.
And their other fingers waving,
To the Southward and the Northward,
To the deep and wide Waitangi,
To the changing Hurunui,
To the gloomy Harewood forest,
To the icy lake of Coleridge,
To the country of Mackenzie,
Chuckling at the favours granted,
Grieving at the little asked for?

Do you ask me whence these chucklings,
What might be these favours granted,
Who these subtle, crafty shepherds,
Who the simple-minded Council,
Statesmen, members, legislators ?
I would answer, I would tell you,
In a pretty little story
Of the very ancient ages.

Oloware, the Secretary,
Sat within the Council chamber,
On the crimson-covered cushions,
On the ministerial benches ;
Pen and ink were placed before him ;
At his side a pile of papers ;
On the floor the bulky blue-books
In his hands before him held he
The 'Amended Regulations.'

Tomicas, the chief surveyor,
Sat upon the seat beside him,
On the crimson-covered cushions,
On the ministerial benches ;
In his hands another copy
Of the Waste Lands Regulations,
The 'Amended Regulations.'

All around the Council Chamber
Sat the six-and-twenty members,
Representing all the people,
All the districts of the Province ;
Christchurch, Kaiapoi, and Avon,
Akaroa and Rakaia,
Ashley, Lyttelton, and Heathcote,
Timaru, and Port Victoria.
In their hands before them held they,
All the six-and-twenty members,
The 'Amended Regulations.'

Rose then Oloware the fluent,
The long-winded Secretary,
Spake such words of sounding grandeur,
Sentences so swift and rapid,
Phrases of such length and glibness,
That the boldest bowed before him,
Stopped his ear-holes with his fingers,
Wished himself outside the chamber.
But to tell you his oration,
All the fervour of his genius,
All his ornamental language,
'Twould be longer, deeper, swifter,
And much harder to get over
Than the Rangitata river.
But, before he ended, spake he
('Twas the pith of his oration):—
"We have thought and deemed it proper
To throw open all the country
By relaxing the conditions
Which have tied it up so closely;
And the Government doth ask ye
To assent to certain measures
(Those Amended Regulations
Ye are holding now before ye)
Which relax the said conditions
That have tied the land so tightly;
Tightly tied it, closely bound it,
From the ready-money buyer.
And the question is before ye,
Under your consideration,
Aye or no, to pass these measures,
The 'Amended Regulations.'"

Thus he spake for twenty minutes,
Making frequent repetitions
And subdued reverberations,
Like the dropping down of water
From a spout in rainy weather
Into some half-empty barrel.

When he stopped rose Jonnioltok,
Shrewd and subtle Jonnioltok,
He the double-barrelled justice,
Ever prompt to give opinions;
And at once he shoved his oar in
In his customary manner —
" I assent to these proposals
With a trifling reservation.
Ye will sweep away conditions,
Justly sweep away restrictions,
Which tie up the land so closely;
Only ye'll except the squatter,
Will not touch the rights of squatters,
Of the shepherds and the stockmen.
Ye shall take the rights of farmers,
Of the millers, bakers, butchers,
Tailors, drapers, clothiers, hatters,
Soldiers, doctors, undertakers,
Of storekeepers and bootmakers,
Of all trades and occupations,
Of all persons in the province,
But the shepherds, the runholders;
Them ye shall not touch nor injure."

Thus he spake, and gave no reason,
Shrewd and subtle Jonnioltok!
But he left the other shepherds,
Squatters, and the friends of squatters,
To uphold him with their reasons;
For his words had done the business,
Woke desires were never dreamed of.
And a flutter passed among them,
Lighting eyes with apprehension,
Opening mouths with expectation,
Consciousness of something coming;
Something of advantage coming;
And they took the hint and followed.

So the parson-bird, the tui,
The white bearded songster tui,
In the morning wakes the woodlands
With his customary music.
Then the other tuis round him
Clear their throats and sing in concert,
All the parson birds together.
And as sheep together huddled
On some river-bed of shingle,
Of Rakaia or Waitangi,
Or the changing Hurunui,
Stand beside the flowing water,
Shrink beside the rapid water,
And refuse to wet their fleeces;
Till one bolder than the others,
Jumbuck of a forward nature,
Takes the stream as if he knew it,
Tells them he knows all about it.
Then the others struggle after,
Struggle and plunge headlong after,
Wondering at their own presumption.
So the shepherds, the runholders,
Followed after Jonnioltok,
Their bell-wether Jonnioltok.

First rose burly Scotje-tomsin,
He the portly, big and bulky,
Round proportioned, talking loudly,
Making little men to tremble
At his violence of language:—
"We will leave the land to squatters;
They may hold it on for ever;
For they build on, and improve it,
Make their houses and their gardens,
Farms, and comfortable homesteads;
And, what's more, they mean to keep it.
Therefore ye must let them keep it,

Ye had better let them have it.
Who is here that will oppose me,
He's a fool and out of order."

Then spoke rugged Bobirodi,
The hard-headed one from Yorkshire,
He the prince of all the squatters,
Largest holder of runholders :—
"Ye remember old Suellis,
Councillor with us of old time ;
Crafty statesman, cunning prophet,
Who taught all of us our wisdom ;
He arranged this matter for us,
And he said it should not alter,
Should remain as he had left it,
As he prophesied, so be it."

And the very big man Stunnem
Moving only eyes and shoulders,
Mutely making demonstrations,
Saying nought, was most impressive.

Then the shepherds in a chorus,
Squatters and the friends of squatters,
Begged, implored, and prayed the Council
To consider all their hardships ;
How their rents were so oppressive,
How their wool was sold for nothing,
How they could not sell their wethers
For the paltry price of mutton,
How the market rate of stations
Showed it was a losing business ;
And they begged and prayed the Council
To maintain the old conditions
That had tied the land so closely
Only on behalf of squatters,
Sweeping quite away the others.

But the most effective reason,
Most conclusive in their favour,
Was the look that passed among them
All around the Council Chamber.

Few were bold enough to argue
In reply to Bobirodi,
To the bulky Scotje-tomsin,
To the very big man Stunnem,
To the subtle Jonnioltok.
And the few that stood their ground there,
Stood their ground and asked for justice,
Simple justice to all classes,
They were bullied and brow-beaten,
Called to order, reprimanded,
By the big men, the stockowners,
Squatters and the friends of squatters,
And the timid ones around them
Who would fain be friends of squatters.
So the fluent Secretary,
Oloware the rapid speaker,
With his colleague sitting by him,
Tomicas, the Chief Surveyor,
Trembled on the crimson cushions,
Gave them all that they demanded,
Granted all the boon they asked for,
Never dared to raise objections,
For they feared the mighty squatters.

Then departed all the stockmen,
Crafty squatters, subtle shepherds,
To the Southward, to the Northward,
To the wide and deep Waitangi,
To the changing Hurunui,
To the gloomy Harewood Forest,
To the icy lake of Coleridge,
To the country of Mackenzie,

To the regions of the Westward;
With their thumbs up to their noses
And their other fingers waving,
Chuckling at the favours granted,
Grieving at the little asked for.

And they kicked the farmer backward
From the fertile spots of country
In the region of the Westward,—
Never thinking of hereafter.

C. W.

February, 1858.

No. 7.

THE SUMNER ROAD. (17)

"His ideas are somewhat above the level."—*Edinburgh Review.*

The bard, a man of dissatisfied mind, on his way over a certain hill, is first impressed by grand historical recollections;

THE Sumner Road! the Sumner Road!
Which burly Thomas first began;
Where Dobson all his skill bestowed,
FitzGerald drove, and Ronnage ran.
Eternal talking still goes on;
But nothing save the talk is done.

But afterwards, by certain melancholy features of the present day.

The gangers and contractor's crews,
The navvy's pick, the ditcher's spade,
Have found the gain your slopes refuse.
On other works is money made—
On lines whose course is further west
Than ever your projectors guessed.

Becoming weary, he rests his body and exercises his imagination.

Mount Pleasant looks on Sumner Bay,
And Sumner Bay looks out to sea.
And, musing there an hour away,
I dreamed that all might yet agree.
For, sitting on Colonial grass,
I could not deem myself an ass.

He recalls the story of one Ronnage, a famous freebooter once, afterwards vanquished, but not without many escapes;

A Peeler sat beside the bank
Where prison kettles boil and fiz:
A score of barrows stood in rank—
A score of felons—all were his.
He counted them that summer's day,
But when he turned they ran away.

And he likens the public to the said Ronnage, in that they are not minded to stay by the road work.

They ran away—And where runn'st thou,
My public ?—On this Sumner Road,
Five hundred drays were toiling now
Had you less flighty conduct showed.
But now—so wealthy have you got
That here ten thousand pounds may rot!

He laments the imbecility of the times, but believes that The Hour is coming, and the Man not far off.

'Tis something in the dearth of sense
Among the present heirs of power,
To feel that I, some short time hence,
Shall have a great and glorious hour;
Shall be the minister of fate
To set these crooked matters straight.

In the meantime, he draws up a petition to the Hon. the Provincial Council, asking for a money grant.

Shall we still crawl o'er mountains steep?
Must we but pack while others cart?
Councillors! of your surplus keep
For our necessities a part!
Of Five Score Thousands grant but Five
To keep the Sumner Road alive!

But no member to whom he applies will present it, alleging Standing Orders as the obstacle; but really, he thinks, fearful of the coming elections.

What! silent Rhodes? and silent Hall?
 Oh, no! Their voices faintly loud,
Sound like a distant baby's squall,
 And answer—"Let one hustings crowd—
But one—pronounce, we'll vote the sum.
'Tis but the public that is dumb."

He then tries out-of-door agitation; but finds that the people of Canterbury are so full of their private concerns

In vain! in vain! strike other cords!
 Fetch in some fresh colonial beer!
Leave roads to Governments and Boards;
 And talk of sheep and oxen here!
Hark! joining in the accustomed strain,
How jaws each joggle-headed swain!

That they won't pay much attention to public affairs.

You have your West Coast Road set out,
 When will your East Coast Road be done?
Of two such works why do without
 The shorter and more useful one?
Fools! would ye win what's worth the winning,
Ye must begin at the beginning.

He thinks to gain credit with some by spouting second-hand the 'Times' against loans to colonies, and getting up a cry against the U.B.A.

Trust not for money to the Banks!
 They make a charge of ten per cent.
Your land, which owes no stranger thanks,
 Is money—more than can be spent.
But banker's charge and banking cost
Is only so much money lost.

But even this does not succeed, and he goes in for the farming interest and the manufacture of beer for export, producing specimens on which he ventures to experiment.

Fill up the glass with native ale!
 Our farmers grew the barley crop;
Our brewers brewed the liquid pale.
 But gazing on its frothless top,
On mine the frigid dews distil,
To think I've got to cross the hill.

But his auditors turn out to be bullock drivers from a sheep station, who have no votes, and prefer brandy to beer—which also disagrees with himself. Overcome by his feelings, he rushes out to return to the town whence he came, cursing the Bridle-path by his gods.

Place me in Papanui swamp;
  Where nothing save some steers and I
Shall hear each other's level tramp;
  There, hill-less, let me live and die!
Climbing is work for donkeys—Here!
Waiter, remove this beastly beer!

C. W.

June, 1859.

Address to the Provincial Council of Canterbury.

AFTER THE HON. MRS. NORTON.

MOVE not! Move not! ye reckless M.P.C.'s!
  Your best framed Bills have many a doubtful phrase;
Clauses with which the public disagrees,
  'Ere they're Gazetted for a few short days.
        Move not! Move not!

Move not! Move not! The Bill you move may drop,
  May be rejected though by you 'tis passed;
His Honor's veto may its progress stop,
  Or Colonel Browne may disallow at last.
        Move not! Move not!

Move not! Move not! The clause you move may change,
  May be amended by a word or two;
The meaning, fondly laboured o'er, grow strange;
  The clause may still be passed, but not by you!
        Move not! Move not!

Move not! Move not! Oh, warning vainly said
  To new-fledged members, of their motions proud!
Bills of his moving turn the poor man's head;
  Legal and faultless—till they're disallowed!
        Move not! Move not!

C. W,

March, 1856.

Where's the Engineer? (1*)

THE autumn time is past its prime;
The winter draws anigh;
The southern rain pours on the plain;
The swamps are rising high;
The drains begin to tumble in;
The bridges want repair;
The roadway cuts in holes and ruts,
And holloas out for care.

With cash opprest the public chest
Is almost overflowed;
In copper coined, 'twould metal find
For fifty miles of road.
The country through there's work to do;
And most this time of year;
But still we stand on every hand,
For—Where's the Engineer?

The cuckoo green, in summer seen,
With shiny plumage drest,
In autumn flies to other skies
Towards the warmer west;
But back he'll wing his way in spring
And stay for half-a-year;
Six months at least he loves the East;
So may the Engineer!

The constant breeze from eastern seas
Across the plain may blow,
Where forest fair and granite bare
Are clad in western snow;
But, fast and warm, the nor'-west storm
Will quit those deserts drear;
And sigh and burn in glad return:
So may the Engineer!

The glorious sun, when day is done,
  Drops on the mountain's crest,
And lends the ray we felt to-day
  To warm and light the west;
But though he sink o'er ocean's brink,
  To-morrow he'll appear
From out the tide the other side,
  So may the Engineer!

But though the bird the West preferred,
  Nor mountain breezes blew;
And though the sun when day is done
  Bade us a last adieu;
Still D——n, thee we hope to see,
  Our longing hearts to cheer;
Still we cry out, with piteous shout,
  Return, Oh Engineer!

For thou must know—what figures show—
  We hold thee *very dear;*
It racks our heart from one to part
  Who's worth so much—a year.
But if the West thou lovest best,
  Nor dost thy duties here—
Then rest thee—stay for aye away—
We only say 'twere cheap to pay
  Another Engineer.

C. W.

May, 1858.

Epigram.

THE NELSON APPEAL. [19]

THE ancient pilgrim on his way
  Took neither purse nor scrip, they say,
Nor gold nor other coin to pay
  The proper charges of the trip.

This precept Nelson half obeys—
Has gold, but yet no charges pays;—
And to her neighbour pilgrims says:—
"We'll share and share alike always;—
I keep my purse, take you my scrip."

C. W.

July, 1858.

Charade of the Times.

"A straight line is the shortest distance between two points."—EUCLID.

MORN on the waters! Purple and bright
Bursts on the billows the flushing of light;
Bright in the beam it has caught from afar,
Sparkles the surge on the Sumner Bar;
Struggling through mists with a mimic wrath,
Gleam the steep slopes of the Bridle Path.
Drooping his eyes, and wringing his hands,
On Lyttelton jetty a Colonist stands;
What shall he do with his Household gods?
His chairs and tables, and curtains, and rods?
Greener than Erin's most verdurous turf,
Shall he trust them to Sumner's treacherous surf?
Or wearily drag them, box and bag,
By Evans' Pass, and Gollan's Crag,
Over the slippery steep Zig-Zag?
Ensphered in the Planet, or Wheeler and Nurs'd,
How! oh, How shall be moved *My First?*

But hark! a voice of cheerful bode—
"FitzGerald has opened the Sumner road!"
Cheerily starts he, with heart elate,
Case, and package, bag, bundle, and crate;
Till he finds, as he nears the Sticking Point,
That the times, and the road, are out of joint.
See these carts of cruel stone;
Hark to the blasters' warning moan!

"Back from our path, ye ill-starred men,
For the Sumner Road is closed again!"
While the Christchurch bell, in mournful mode,
Tolls *My Last* for the Sumner Road;
And seems to foretell its own sad fate
To the Colonist and his luckless freight.

Hurrah, for the cure of all our ills!
Hurrah, for the triumph of sturdy wills!
Double and treble our exports grow;
Northward, and southward, and westward, ho!
Shall the stream of population flow;
Its Halcyon days our land shall know;
When free from fear of tempest or tide,
My Whole shall pierce the green hill side.

October, 1859.

The Emmigrant's Carol for Christmas.

OH, Christmas! merry Christmas!
We hail thee once again,
To shores where late thy cheering morn
Ne'er dawned on Christian men.
But from their thrones for evermore
The heathen gods are flung;
And the good old Christmas tide is hail'd
In the good old English tongue.

But not, as in the olden land,
Where still our memories cling,
By blazing hearths, amid the snow,
Our Christmas songs we sing.
But when the bright sun's soften'd rays
Are with the flowers at play,
We cull sweet summer's fruits to grace
Our board, on Christmas Day.

The children in the green lanes bind
The roses in their hair,
And the sad old year goes sighing out,
To leave a scene so fair;
While friends meet friends with happy hearts
In many a social band,
To hold their merry Christmas
In our adopted land.

A. C.

December, 1859.

The Town and the Torrent. ([20])

A RECKLESS RHYME.

"Rusticus expectat dum defluat amnis, at ille
Labitur, et labetur in omne volubilis ævum."—HORACE.

THERE'S a town that bears a grand old name,
Though it be but a new made spot;
The beauty that some other towns may claim
Every one knows it has not.
With its dead bare level, and square cut streets,
Its houses so scattered and small;
And the wind that will blow, and the sand that won't go,
'Tis not pleasant to live in at all.
But 'twas once a good business, I understand,
Buying and selling the Christchurch land.

(AIR—"Duncan Gray.")

Christchurch lies a little low;
Hey, hey, the level o't!
Above the tide a foot or so;
Hey, hey, the level o't.
And when about the town you go,
Sundry indications show
That here a river used to flow;
Hey, and that's the —— o't!

Only think, here's a go;
Fancy that years ago—
I don't like to make it too short or too long;
A very safe venture is
Several centuries—
The learned must pardon me if I go wrong;
My only apology
Is that geology
Was not a science they taught me when young.
But, if asked what Christchurch is on,
Sir Roderick Murchison
Would, fearless of heresies,
Say, from those terraces,
Sandhills and shingle lines running along,
That, in reality,
Down this locality
Some torrent had come it uncommonly strong.

(Air—" Cork Leg.")

At Avonhead lived one Mister Bray,
Who every morning used to say
"I should not be much surprised to-day
If Christchurch city were swept away,
By the rushing, crushing, flushing, gushing,
Waimakariri river."

He told his tale, and he showed his plan,
How the levels lay, and the river ran;
The neighbours thought him a learned man,
But wished him further than Ispahan,
With his wearing, tearing, flaring, scaring,
Waimakariri river.

(Air—" Kitty of Coleraine.")

As young Mr. Rowley one morning was going
With a barrel on wheels to the river for drink,
Instead of a mile off, he found it was flowing
Five yards from the house, and a foot from the brink.

The river was tumbling, the banks they were crumbling,
  Poor Rowley had scarcely got time to jump round,
When very soon after, from basement to rafter,
  The whole of his house disappeared from the ground.

AIR—("Froggy would a-wooing go.")

So off he jumped, and took to his heels,
    Heigh-ho! says Rowley;
So off he jumped, and took to his heels,
And off went the bullock and barrel on wheels,
    From the rolling, bowling Waimakariri.
      "Heigh-ho!" says young Mister Rowley.

And when he came to Christchurch town!
    "Heigh-ho!" says Rowley;
And when he came to Christchurch town,
"Look out," says he, "for the coming down
    Of the rolling, bowling Waimakariri."
      "Heigh-ho!" says young Mister Rowley.

The people all got in a terrible fright,
    At the heigh-ho! of Rowley;
The people all got in a terrible fright,
And went by dozens to take a sight
    At the rolling, bowling Waimakariri—
      "Oh, do," says young Mister Rowley.

Prompt were the steps the Government took.
The Superintendent closed his book,
And started rapidly up from where he
    Just then sat,
    Called for his hat,
And stepped at once to the Secretary.
That eminent officer, just before,
  Being always ready alike for pleasure or
Business, had shut and locked his door,
  And stepped with the news to his friend the Treasurer.

The man of money had hurriedly gone—
  So said his feminine attendant—
With a couple of swimming belts tied on,
  Across to His Honor the Superintendent.

First up, then down,
Then across the town
The three went, one another following,
Like wolves in a cage,
Till they got in a rage,
Which they'd very great trouble indeed in swallowing.
They certainly would have walked till night—
They might have been going till morning light;
They might have been playing the whole of the week
A triangular game of hide and seek;
They might have been walking, in imitation
Of the cork leg's wonderful peregrination,
I can't tell how,
Even till now—
A striking example of quick and dead,
The constant, heavy, monotonous tread,
Leaving intact both body and head,
But wearing out the soul,
And making each corporeal whole
A "corporation sole"—
Not fleshless spirits, of which there are hosts,
But the very *vice versâ* of ghosts;
Spiritless bodies, that should be the grave in,
Of whom I have known no example, save in
The first navigation concern of the Avon.

This trio walked—*before* they died—
With swinging arms, and lengthened stride,
And nose aloft in air;
With head erect, and open-eyed,
And backward streaming hair;
They strode the street of still Madras,
Where grows at will the untrodden grass,
To Sumner road the wide.

Thence on by Cashel's peopled street,
Some of whose houses almost meet
In ranks down either side.
To where, cool gliding through the heat,
Slides Avon's silvery tide.
And as adown the stream he pressed,
Each turned a glance towards the west,
Dreaming of quick disaster;
And saw, or thought he saw, or guessed
He saw the billows' foaming crest;
Then stepped a little faster.
By Gloucester's half-worn thoroughfare,
Whose panes with every product glare—
Soft goods, and hard, and holloware,
With Stringer's buns and toffees;
And Cookham's famous boots are there,
So is the Union Office.

By street and by terrace each hurried apace,
One after the other, but all in vain,
Till they reached the right reverend Martyr's place,
And then they began the round again.
For it happened perversely, as things will chance,
With the luck to which most poor mortals born are,
As each round a turning gave a first glance,
His man was doubling a distant corner.

Now they might have walked, as I said before,
A day, or a week, or a month, or more;
But happily, as they were going at score,
THE CLOCK STRUCK FOUR!

Witches, we know, and fairies too,
And every supernatural crew,
In the height of their dance, when the cock does crow,
Instantly stop
The nocturnal hop,
Vanish in air, and away they go!

So public officials of every degree,
Though slaves at fifty-nine minutes past three,
The instant they hear the stroke of four
The pen must stop,
And the paper must drop;
The books are shut, and they work no more.
Quick and far, with electric force,
'Twas felt; the Government stopped, of course,
No need of clock, nor of bell for them;
Instinct told them 'twas 4 p.m.
Each, as if shot,
Stopped on the spot,
Turned on his heel, gave his forehead a wipe;
Felt in his pocket aud pulled out a pipe;
Got ready to smoke, and prepared to depart,
Slowly, in search of some ale, to the Hart,
Now looking the map in,
You'll find it would happen,
Each coming up from a different beat,
That just at the junction they would meet
Of Cathedral square with Hereford street.

First and at once, by right of his station,
His Honor demanded an explanation:
"I say—I say—
"Nice fellows, you two,
"Running away,
"Just when you knew there was something to do.
"But go—I say, go!
"I want dinner—you know
"I'm hungry, you made me run after you so.
"But stay—I say, stay!
"One of you call on the clerk on your way—
"You see that the river is
"Getting mysterious, p'rhaps even serious,
"It's a chance if to-morrow we all are alive—
"And let him deliver his

"Summonses all my advisers to call,
"To hold an Executive Council at five.
"And here—I say, here!
"Remind him to summon the Engineer."

They met—'twas up a stair—for they thought it was coming;
They looked—it was not there—but they heard like its humming.
They talked in whisper'd tone, their keen anguish to smother;
But one, and one alone, said 'twas all his grandmother!
What's to be done?
Was the general question—
Felt, but unspoken;
Till suddenly one
Made a suggestion,
And silence was broken.
He began by observing that all propriety
Showed that in every novel society
Naught should be done at all at variance
With the dictates of old experience.
That mention made he
Of a sage old lady—
Her name would be recognised far and wide,
Who, when ocean invading
Set other folks wading,
Made use of a pitchfork to stop the tide.
And then he proposed, as the easiest plan
(In talking of forks he, of course, the most simple meant)
For stopping the river, that every man
Should furnish himself with a similar implement.
Another sage Councillor rose up to say,
With his colleague's opinion he partly accorded;
But, seeing the progress of science each day,
Some room for improvement was surely afforded,
He thought that, laying aside the prong,
Whose only use was on shallow beaches,
The pole by itself, six times as long,
Would be better in currents and rapid reaches.

The members approved the latter suggestion;
They put and carried, *nem. con.*, the question;
And, dropping irrelevant conversation,
Agreed to the following

PROCLAMATION!

WHEREAS it seems likely the river may break
Through its banks; and we know not the course it may take;
And whereas 'tis expedient to run up some better a
Rampart: Now therefore, I, William, *et cetera*,
Proclaim that all persons shall institute searches
For pitchforks, and all they can find they must purchase;
Then knock all the prongs off, and taking the staves away,
March to the river and help keep the waves away.
Done at our palace, September sixteen,
The year does not matter, and

GOD SAVE THE QUEEN!

Odd, very odd it was thought by all;
  Uncommonly odd the Government thought it.
So fancies a cricketer dropping a ball,
  Precisely the moment he thinks he has caught it.
    Most provoking! beyond all joking!
    Very perplexing! exceedingly vexing!
In spite of their skill, and in spite of their science;
    In spite of the fame
    Of the eminent dame,
On whose old appliance they placed such reliance;
    The rampart of sticks
    When they managed to fix,—
And far from too easy a matter they found it,—
    The stream, rising frightfully,
    Broke, as if spitefully,
Over it, under it, through it, and round it.

More frightened than ever, the folks on the plains
Turned, after they heard it, uncommonly brown
In all the nor'-westers and easterly rains,
For fear that the river might chance to come down.
While some men who thought themselves *extra* sagacious
And offered to bet on it many a crown,
To make their opinion the more efficacious,
Affirmed that the river would surely come down.
But to silence for ever all empty conjecture,
To settle all doubts on the fate of the town,
The highest authority proved in a lecture,
By figures and facts, that it *must* come down.
From that time to this, says the story, the river
Showed such disregard for all reason that by it you'd
Judge it had studied the journals, and ever
Remained in its bed with remarkable quietude.

C. W.

April, 1860.

Ode to New Zealand.

A GROWL IN A SOU'-WESTER.

EDEN of the Southern Sea,
I devote my lay, to thee,
Thee, of whom at Home they tell
Things to make the bosom swell.
Thee, of whom in Crosby square
Loud laudations shake the air:
(Disbelieve what mortal can
The seductive tongue of Gann?)
So that men have christened thee,
Eden of the Southern Sea.

Thee whom, praised by magic *lyre*
Of Hursthouse, men unseen admire!
Land of plains and grassy swells,
Where the gentle Maori dwells,
Equal, save in copper face,
With the European race,
Strong in love, in council grave,
Christian, chivalrous, and brave;
These are things they tell of thee,
Eden of the Southern Sea.

Where the bee, on drooping wing,
Laden with the spoils of spring,
Lays up so profuse a store,
Suffices all, and something more;
Where the breezes, soft and free,
Rival those of Italy.
Where the lovely ka-ka screeches,
And the pigs are fed on peaches!
What on earth compares with thee,
Eden of the Southern Sea?

Where the wide extended plain
Waves with fields of golden grain;
Where the shepherd, 'midst his sheep,
Beneath the stars fears not to sleep;
Where the zephyrs from the hills
Are med'cine for all human ills;
Where contentment reigns around;
And no murmurers can be found:
This, and more, they say of thee,
Eden of the Southern Sea.

But 'tis sad, though very clear,
That we're fated now to hear,
Landed on thy far-famed shore,
Things we heard not named before.

Settlers arming for their lives
And their little ones and wives
Forced to fly, or stay and be
"Chawed up catawampously!"
  We were not told this of thee,
  Eden of the Southern Sea.

Land where men with brains of fog
Built a city in a bog!
Land of rain, and storm, and flood!
Land of water, wind, and mud!
Where six days a week the gale,
Laden thick with rain or hail,
First from sou'-west blows a piercer,
Then veers nor'-west and blows fiercer!
  This is what I think of thee,
  Eden of the Southern Sea.

Land where all is dear and bad,
Comfort scarcely to be had;
Wooden house, with shingle roof,
Neither wind nor waterproof;
And the mutton and the beef
Fit to cause a Briton grief;
And of all things the most dear
(As to price) a glass of beer!
  Oh! I'm sadly sold in thee,
  Eden of the Southern Sea.

But I have located here;
No alternative, I fear,
But to make the best of thee,
Only longing to be free;
Patiently to bear thy clime,
And anticipate the time
When, my transportation o'er,
I shall seek some genial shore,
  Never to return to thee,
  Eden of the Southern Sea.

J. T. R.

July, 1860.

Album Lines.

THE BAZAAR.

OF all the wicked modes whereby
  Weak men are circumvented,
Supreme is the Bazaar, say I,
  In evil hour invented.

You go, perchance, to view the scene
  Most strictly a spectator ;
The times of late so bad have been,
  You're *not* a speculator.

With purse well guarded, heart of flint,
  And eyes of cold abstraction,
You callous seem to every hint,
  And blind to each distraction.

Of caps at home you've quite a store,
  Of neck-ties also plenty,
You reckon slippers by the score,
  Of vests at least have twenty.

In cushions, markers, studs, and rings,
  Your stock is most extensive,
Why buy pen-wipers ? useless things !
  Outrageously expensive !

Rash man ! though these you may elude,
  Strange goods will take their places ;
Think not that here you can intrude,
  And treat with scorn the Graces.

Those little socks for tiny feet,
  You homeward soon will carry,
The baby's dress should be complete ;—
  Who knows but you may marry ?

In vain you plead, with long-drawn face,
You want no parasol;
The nymph holds forth with winning grace
The witcheries of a doll!

Hot and oppressed, you seek the seat
Near lemonade and ices,
Where gingerbread and bon-bons meet,
And sell at fearful prices.

Here for awhile you seek repose,—
Alas! a vain illusion!
A Psyche, while the nectar flows,
O'erwhelms you with confusion.

Who loses money feels the smart;
Some friend may money lend us;
Worse ill works Cupid's subtle dart,
From which, kind Heaven, defend us!

J. T. R.

October, 1860.

Arcades Ambo. ([21])

A BUCOLIC—AFTER VIRGIL.

First Swain.—FITZGERALD! once again we meet!
Thee warmly doth the country greet!
If thou to me assistance lend,
Then I will be thy dearest friend.

Second Swain.—Oh, Moorhouse! Fortune's favor'd son!
Thou hast her every gift but one.
If to my counsels thou'lt attend,
I'll make thee great and be thy friend.

First Swain.—Nay, Fitz, I fear thou hast forgot
That I'm in power, and thou art not;
My plans are formed, take that for granted,
And keep advice until 'tis wanted.

Second Swain.—Oh! Moorhouse, Moorhouse, half an ounce
Of sense is worth a pound of bounce;
Be wise: thy reckless schemes resign,
And wholly trust to me and mine.

First Swain.—Now, harken! rather, I declare,
Than give our fortunes to thy care—
Rather than trust thy plans or thee—
I'd sink the country in the sea.

Second Swain.—Then harken thou! in loud debate,
With warning voice throughout the State,
I'll rouse the bitter social storm,
To do thee and thy projects harm.

First Swain.—Begone, and do thy worst; for I
Thee and thy crack-brained schemes defy.

Second Swain.—Begone! and let the public try
Which is more crack-brained, thou or I.

First Swain.—But stay—perhaps—conceive—suppose
The public *will not* come to blows.

Second Swain.—Aye, stay—perhaps they may not quite
For either schemer care to fight.

First Swain.—Of course they think you very rash.

Second Swain.—And you, they know, can scatter cash.

First Swain.—But then, you're at the bottom true.

Second Swain.—Well, come! they think the same of you.

Both.—No quarrels, then; the public know
That they themselves are rather slow,
And wish that you—and I—who lead,
Should have a little extra speed.

[*Exeunt amicably.*

C. W.

December, 1860.

The First of May.

WHEN first I saw young Neddy,
'Twas on the first of May;
On a slashing mare to town he rode,
His yearly rent to pay.
But when that mare was out at grass
For six weeks in the spring,
No blade was there that could compare
With the nice young man I sing.
As he rode on his spanking mare,
By the corner of Milliner's square,
Every girl in the place dropped ribbons and lace,
And looked after the spanking pair.

In high Provincial Council,
The Members brave and wise,
Sit silent round, without a sound,
When the speaker "Order" cries.
But Neddy, more imperious,
Makes all round him shout.

As he passes them by, they stare and cry
"Does your mother know you're out!"
As he gallops his slashing mare
The lads all cry "Take care,"
"Hold on as you ride"—"Take a place inside;"
Or, "Come down off that spanking mare."

Young Neddy round his hat, Sir,
Has a whisp of muslin green;
But the tradesmen folk who trust him
More verdant are, I ween;
For he looks so youthful, so mild and truthful,
With a sweet engaging air,
They never ask payment for food or raiment,
But give it as free as air.
As he mounts his spanking mare,
They rush to their doors and stare,
And envy together the woolliest wether
That's shorn for him and his mare.

I'd rather own that mare, sir,
With a hempen halter tied,
Than a ship-load down from Melbourne town,
With saddles and all beside.
For the agent would call to-morrow,
With a little account to pay,
But Neddy, the thief, would have come to grief,
And be galloping out of the way,
On another spanking mare,
While all his creditors swear
That there's plenty to lose, if to trust you choose,
A man with a spanking mare.

C. W.

May, 1861.

The Lament of Canterbury. ([22])

DEAR Mr. Editor, I pray give ear
To my sad tale, my pitiful lament;
I've not been so annoy'd this many a year,
My inside's really quite in a ferment.
Those other provinces—oh dear!—oh dear!
Are filling me with shame and discontent;
I, who was once so vigorous and bold,
And in the dumps—and why? *I've got no gold!*

There's that Otago—oatmeal eating place—
Is turning gold up by the hundred weight.
That fag-end of the world—now in the race,
Is going ahead at a confounded rate.
See what a grin lights up each Scotchman's face,
When they compare their own with my sad fate.
Otago may be bleak, and wet, and cold,
But what of that, when they've got lots of gold?

Then up at Nelson, too, they've still got patches,
Where men may earn about a crown a day;
And every month you hear of folks in batches,
To some new gully being led away.
Though their best fields are only chicken's scratches,
And their best claims were never known to pay.
But I don't dare to speak lest I get told,—
"We have got *some*; but *you*—you've got *no* gold!"

There's the North Island, too, if people knew it,
Has got gold from the one end to the other;
See Coromandel, how the stuff runs through it,
If Mr. Maori would but act the brother,
And let his white companion get up to it,—
If it was here, I'd soon stop all that bother.
We know not what the future may unfold.
But I'm afraid it will bring me no gold.

I've got a great geologist to look
About for gold and try can he discern it;
And he's been fossicking in every nook,
But nothing found, or I should quickly learn it—
Except some coal, as black as any rook,
And famous fuel, if one could only burn it.
Coal is a mine of wealth, as I've been told;
But blow black diamonds! What I want is gold!

I've boundless plains (half swamp, half stony land);
I've mighty streams that through those plains come-roaring;
I've lots of bush (though it's not close at hand);
I've lofty hills—through one of them I'm boring;
I've foaming cataracts, and glaciers grand,
Though I don't think such places worth exploring;
I've stores of mineral wealth, as yet untold,
But none of what I want—I've got no gold!

I've circulated rumours, not a few,
Of people finding nuggets by the score,
To cause a rush, but that game wouldn't do,
It only got me laughed at more and more.
They found some lately down at Timaru—
Though they that found it planted it before.
The people don't seem willing to be sold—
They can't be made believe there's any gold!

What shall I do? My case is very hard.
I've one more grief to state before I leave it.
I'm offering now One Thousand Pounds Reward
For finding gold—*but people don't believe it!*
They think—the beggars are so on their guard—
It's all a hoax, and that they'll not receive it.
Dear Mr. Editor, may I be so bold,
One question—Do you know of any gold?

J. T. M.

October, 1862.

The Lost Steamship. [23]

SLOWLY the great red sun
Sank in the seas;
Grey cloud grey cloud upon,
Ossa on Pelion,
Up from the horizon
Crept on the breeze,
That with a mournful sigh,
Like a sad spirit's cry,
Weirdly and fitfully
Swept o'er the seas.

Then—while the heavens grew
Deeper and deeper blue,
Changing to ebon hue—
Star after star,
Climbing the distant height,
Each a pale thread of light
Down through the murky night
Shot from afar.

Still the great clouds of grey
Darker and darker, aye,
Over the starry way
Rose on the breeze.
Darker and darker yet,
Till over all they met,
And, like a pall of jet,
Hung o'er the seas.

Silence—unbroken by
Aught but the sea-bird's cry,
And the wind's solemn sigh;
Saving the sound
Of the great inky waves,
Rising o'er ocean caves,
Falling o'er ocean graves—
Reigned all around.

See! where a stream of light
Gleams from a furnace bright,
Beams through the gloom of night.
Over the deep.
Yonder a steamer's bound;
Hark to the engine's sound;
Hark how the wheels go round,
Merrily sweep.

Gaily the waters splash,
Gaily the paddles clash,
As through the waves they dash
Swiftly along.
And o'er the rolling seas,
Comes on the fitful breeze,
Mingled with sounds like these,.
Laughter and song.

Hark! what is that I hear?
Hush, 'tis a sound of fear!
Strain now the eye and ear,
The Light is gone.
Oh! List that dreadful cry,
Like a last agony;
In it what terrors lie,
God! that 'twere dawn!

Hark! o'er the murky main
Comes the dread sound again;
Yet the eye looks in vain.
Hush, it is o'er.
Now doth a stillness reign,
Save the wind's sigh again,
And the great mournful main
Sobbing to shore.

* * * * *
* * * * *.

Slowly the night has passed,
And the great sun at last
Over the sea has cast
Brightly his ray;
But o'er the rolling deep
Vainly the eye doth sweep;
Nowhere a paddle ship
Speeds on her way.

Vainly the loved ones wait,
Sadly and desolate;
Still is that steamer's fate
Hidden in gloom;
And God alone can tell
What on that night befell,
And how the "City" went
Down to her doom.

Weep for the desolate!
Weep for the widow's state!
Weep for the orphan's fate!
Weep ye and pray
That the great God, who gave
Theirs to one common grave,
Will, in His mercy, save
Them in their day;

And with his favour bless
Widow and fatherless,
Giving to them the grace
Humbly to say—
E'en from beside the grave—
Blessed be God who gave,
And in His wisdom hath
Taken away.

W. J. S.

June, 1865.

The Runaways. (24)

AN HISTORICAL BALLAD.

THERE was an Island in the sea,
  Of which some people say
It was not very wise or old,
  Although its head was GREY.

Now in this Island all the men
  Fell out, as it was found,
Into a quarrel, though it was
  Pacific all around.

For of the people some were black,
  And others they were white;
Which was a serious difference,
  So they began to fight.

One morn they fought, the fight was hot,
  Although the day was show'ry;
And many a gallant soldier then
  Was bid *Memento Maori.*

The smoke was thick, the blacks fell down
  Upon the ground like rain;
Though once they joined a rising, now
  They'll never rise again.

And where the fire was very hot,
  It made a number cold;
It broke the ranks, it melted them,
  And cast them on the mould.

Among the wounded was a man,
  To whom the names belong
Of ENOCH CÆSAR PALMERSTON,
  Done into Maori tongue.

Now Enoch's leg had got in it
  A bullet from a gun;
And when he tried to cut away,
  The wound began to run.

And since he could not run with it,
  He stopped and bound his scars;
And though not hoping to be paid,
  Was pitched upon by Tars.

Who seeing Enoch so cast down,
  They took him up so short;
Said they "You are our prisoner,
  So you must come to Court."

Said he, "I've got a ball inside,"—
  He did not mean to scoff—
"I'll go to Court, and you may then
  Present and let me off."

"No, no!" replied the Boatswain's mate,
  "Avast a bit, my hearty!
Let's see the ball"—but as he spoke,
  They saw another party.

A party of Militia-men,
  An officer therewith;
In camp he was a Corporal Jones,
  In town a general smith.

This Corporal had a warlike nose,
  Gunpowdery in hue;
It Trumpeted his honours, but
  It could not beat tattoo.

For Enoch's face was lined throughout
  With ornamental scars
Of blue, with red ones added in
  The Taranaki wars.

The first were cunning chisel marks,
  The second, crooked ruts;
Proofs, like the *Witness* journal, of
  Essays on Gold, with cuts.

This Jones took Enoch to the camp,
  Where were a number more
Of Maoris, whom his comrades bold
  Made prisoners before.

The General stood in front of them,
  As upright as a larch;
And, though November was the month,
  He sent them off to march.

He sent them all on board a hulk,
  Abreast of Auckland town:
He put them down the hold, and bade
  The soldiers hold them down.

Some snivelled, going in; some howled;
  Some noses blew, with bellows;
But careful keeping in the hulk,
  Soon made them hulking fellows.

Potatoes, bread, and milk, and meat,
  Such was their commissariat.
Tobacco, to assuage their woe;
  And Doctor's stuff, to vary it.

At first they wanted bracing up,
  Their clothes so hung about;
But when they'd been a month on board,
  They wanted letting out.

And so they got a run a-shore,
  For souls' and bodies' profit,
On Kawau's copper beach. Of course,
  They cut their sticks from off it.

For Titus White who guarded them,
He left them on the shore;
Says he, "They've got no boat, nor gear,
Except the copper ore;

"Therefore, they cannot leave the Isle."
And at his joke he laughed;
But, silly Titus White! he quite
Forgot their native craft.

And so by night they ran away,
And got upon the main.
And in the morning Titus went
To fetch them back again.

At last he found them on a hill,
All fortified about.
They hollowed rifle pits within;
And White he holloaed out.

And at his shout, so loud and long—
It was a wondrous sight—
Two hundred dusky faces, then,
Were turned at once to White.

"Come back"—he cried—"my prisoners!"
Each hand directly rose,
And, with extended fingers, gave
Point to their silent noes.

"Come back unto your Governor;
He will avenge your slights.
For Grey's the only medium
Between the Blacks and Whites."

Said they—"No, no! that's very fine;
But Grey will never do.
He is not black enough for us
Nor white enough for you."

Said WHITE—" You are his children dear,
And don't he love you, rather ?
So be advised, and leave your pa,
And come unto your father."

" Perhaps," they said, " we were his sons,
But now we're better nursed.
We're Royal Maori Infantry,
And will see him farther first."

Now TITUS WHITE was puzzled quite,
And knew not what to say ;
So went and told his tale, so blue,
Unto his head, SIR GREY.

" Go back, go back,"—replied his chief,
With sternness on his tongue,—
" They are our rebel prisoners,
Deserving to be hung.

" But tell them "—here he smiled so sly—
" To make them come the quicker,
I'll heap upon them chains of—land
And keep them tight in—liquor."

So TITUS WHITE went back to tell
His chief's determination ;
With Native Office notes which formed
A very free translation.

" I and SIR GEORGE, we love you well,
Like brothers of your race.
We'll swear we do, till we're as black
As you are in the face.

" You shall be found in meat and drink,
Houses and gardens too ;
And make believe you're prisoners,
By having nought to do."

"Give land!" they said, "'Tis all our own.
Do nought;—we do it now!
Give meat!—We shan't be hungry while
A settler owns a cow.

"But if you must have prisoners,
You'll soon accomplish that:
Catch them when starving, and you may
Detain them till they're fat.

"Treat them like us, and do again
The same good natured thing;
Recruit the Maori forces for
His Majesty the King."

C. W.

APPENDIX.

Song before Session (1865.) (1)

(WITH MR. PUNCH'S ACKNOWLEDGMENTS TO THE LONDON "CHARIVARI.")

THE Session is coming, oh dear, oh dear!
The Session is coming, oh dear!
Will there be any fun
Shot with our witty gun?
In the Council preserves this year!

The Super is coming, oh dear, oh dear!
The Super is coming, oh dear!
With pellucid diction,
Some fact and some fiction,
To make up a tale of the year.

Big Rolleston's coming, oh dear, oh dear!
Big Rolleston's coming, oh dear!
With stiffest of phrases
Soliciting praises
For cutting off hospital beer.

Johnny Hall is coming, oh dear, oh dear!
Johnny Hall is coming, oh dear!
To wade through the puddle
Of his West Coast muddle:
With an Act to make the way clear.

Moorhouse is coming, oh dear, oh dear!
Moorhouse is coming, oh dear!
Involved, egotistical,
Forcible, mystical
Speeches more happy than clear.

Herr Tancred is coming, oh dear, oh dear!
  Herr Tancred is coming, oh dear!
    To prove education
    Is best for the nation,
Enforced by a tax and a jeer.

Murray-Aynsley is coming, oh dear, oh dear!
  Murray-Aynsley is coming, oh dear!
    In commerce and shipping
    He won't be found tripping;
He'll tell them much more than they'll hear.

George Buckley is coming, oh dear, oh dear!
  George Buckley is coming, oh dear!
    Great Melbourne parading,
    Its tricks and its trading;
He wants us to copy it here.

Dr. Turnbull is coming, oh dear, oh dear!
  Dr. Turnbull is coming, oh dear!
    With language jocose
    He'll exhibit a dose
To make all the members feel queer.

Old Shand, he is coming, oh dear, oh dear!
  Old Shand, he is coming, oh dear!
    To cock up his bristles
    At spreading of thistles,
If Government won't interfere.

Little Fyfe is coming, oh dear, oh dear
  Little Fyfe is coming, oh dear!
    To know on what principle,
    Interest Municipal
Must suffer for money this year.

The Nabob is coming, oh dear, oh dear!
The Nabob is coming, oh dear!
With Indian story,
In which all the glory
Was gained by a gent from Cashmere.

Mr. Ross isn't coming, oh dear, oh dear!
Mr. Ross isn't coming, oh dear!
Charming propriety,
Grave to satiety,
Where shall we find his compeer?

Mr. Rowe may be coming, oh dear, oh dear!
Mr. Rowe may be coming, oh dear!
To present a petition,
And make requisition
For money to lengthen a pier.

Ollivier's coming, oh dear, oh dear!
Ollivier's coming, oh dear!
Of place he's no seeker,
So make him the Speaker,
To cut off long speeches on beer.

Cabbage Wilson is coming, oh dear, oh dear!
Cabbage Wilson is coming, oh dear!
With speech softly flowing,
Ten to one he'll be blowing
Of the wonderful pile he's made here.

Joe Beswick is coming, oh dear, oh dear!
Joe Beswick is coming, oh dear!
To yawn in Committee,
And think what a pity
The Bills are so long and so drear.

John Peacock is coming, oh dear, oh dear!
  John Peacock is coming, oh dear!
    So bashfully shrewd,
    And so pleasantly rude,
His speeches are short, but they're queer.

Mark Stoddart is coming, oh dear, oh dear!
  Mark Stoddart is coming, oh dear!
    He'll be sure to look out
    For a grant for some trout,
And nice little salmon to rear.

The Majors are coming, oh dear, oh dear!
  The Majors are coming, oh dear!
    To take care of their runs,
    And to beg for big guns;
Amen, say each gay Volunteer.

Geraldine he is coming, oh dear, oh dear!
  Geraldine he is coming, oh dear!
    With much hesitation
    About separation,
Uncertain which course he shall steer.

Mr. Punch is coming, look out, look out!
  Mr. Punch is coming, look out!
    With his baton to whack
    Every silly one's back,
And make them mind what they're about.

VARIORUM.

What Does Lawyer Louis Say? (2)

(A MILD REMONSTRANCE FROM AN UNLEARNED MAN.)

I USED to lead a happy life,
  For many a merry year;
My days were spent apart from strife,
  My nights without a fear.

My world has been a world of play;
  And I, a child of song.
But what does Lawyer Louis say?
  "All's altogether wrong."

I lived a peaceful citizen;
  Paid every rate and tax;
And only growled if, now and then,
  Collectors would'nt wait.
I always thought I *had* to pay,
  Because the law was strong.
But what does Lawyer Louis say?
  "That's altogether wrong."

I loved a blithe and beauteous lass;
  A gentle "Yes" she said.
Love made the moments quickly pass,
  Till Bess and I were wed.
We thought that we were bound that day
  For all our lifetime long.
But what does Lawyer Louis say?
  "That's altogether wrong."

I bought a little piece of land,
  And built our humble cot;
A happy future life we planned,
  And blessed our rural lot.
I thought, perhaps these acres may
  Unto my heirs belong.
But what does Lawyer Louis say?
  "That's altogether wrong."

I'll leave my land, I'll leave my home,
  I'll leave my loving wife;
Through savage foreign lands I'll roam,
  And lead a lawless life.
This world's no more a world of play,
  Nor I a child of song;
For what does Lawyer Louis say?
  "All's altogether wrong."

C. W.

Nursery Rhymes for Political Babies. (3)

I.

HUSHABY BEALEY! O'er the hill top;
When the road's made, in office you'll stop:
When the road isn't made, people will bawl,
"Down with the Government, Bealey and all!"

II.

GOVERNOR GREY
Has little to say,
Since we sent Freddy Weld to mind him;
Don't let him alone,
And he'll go home,
And leave all his blunders behind him.

C. W.

Abridged Edition of the History of the New Zealand War.

SIR DUNCAN CAMERON, with ten thousand men,
Came out from Home, and then went back again.

A Bequest on the Battle-field.

(ADJUSTED FROM SIR WALTER SCOTT.)

CHARGE, BEALEY, charge! On, Moorhouse, on!
Were the last words of Rolleston.

Some of the Affecting Adventures of Poor Cock Canterbury (4)

(BEING A NEW BURDEN TO AN OLD LAY.)

WHO is the Governor?
I am, says Punch,
With my wallet and hunch,
I am the Governor!

Who is the Superintendent?
I am, says Bealey,
O yes, I think really
That I'm the Superintendent.

Who juggles the finances?
I do, says Hall,
With my cup and ball,
I juggle the finances.

Who won't pay the charwoman?
I won't, says Rolleston;
I've banished the holystone,
And I won't pay the charwoman.

Who snubs the schoolmasters?
I do, says Tancred,
For authority I hankered,
So I snub the schoolmasters.

Who'll win the Rakaia?
I will, says Stevens,
At odds and at evens,
I'll win the Rakaia.

Who'll sell the diggers?
I will, says Sale;
You may go bail,
I'll sell the diggers.

Who'll build a tramway?
I will, says White,
Oh, blow me tight!
I'll build a tramway.

Who'll furnish the money?
We will, says the Executive;
By instalments consecutive,
We'll furnish the money.

Who'll bamboozle the People?
I will, says the *Press*;
You must confess
I can bamboozle the People.

A Road Song.

MAKE the road, Johnny, my dear Johnny!
Make the road Johnny, my little man!
Anywhere, anyhow, over the mountains;
Do it as quickly, my boy, as you can.

We are all of us longing, my dear Johnny!
Everything everywhere is all awry.
If you cannot save us, my little manny,
Somebody else must have a try.

No doubt you'll do it; that's if you choose to;
Nobody doubts your powers a bit.
But do it smartly, my little Johnny,
Or soon I'll be writing your *hic jacet*.

Essence of Provincial Council.

SOLEMN body! Sacred spot!
Lukewarm; neither cold nor hot.
Clerk, half nodding, drops a blot.
Opposition talking rot,
How the country goes to pot.

Government, regarding not,
Driving on their old jog-trot.
Members, independent lot,
Sitting, caring not a jot;
Voting, for they know not what,
Money that they have'nt got.
Solemn body! Sacred spot!

Rolleston's Farewell. ([5])

AIR—"Good-bye, Sweetheart."

THE steam is up; the engine's starting.
As you will venture down the line,
The time has come, my mates for parting;
You on your carriage, I on mine.
For if your necks you must be breaking,
I won't go with you; no. not I.
My donkey cart and leave I'm taking;
Good-bye, my mates, good-bye!

You used to vow to me you wouldn't
Attempt such fast designs at all.
You used to swear you would be prudent,
And never climb lest you might fall.
But now for public favour striving,
You won't have me for your ally:
I'd rather our old cart be driving,
Good-bye, my mates, good-bye?

A Choice.

JOHN HALL, he leads a happy life,
In Government Buildings free from strife;
Supreme o'er Road Boards there he rules,
And works his will with other tools.

His power can give us Roads to go
To the West Coast or Jericho;
Or if it likes him not, he'll stay
All traffic to the River Grey.

With bridges he our rivers spans,
Accepts or vetos people's plans;
New Public Office schemes directs,
And costly railway lines selects.

The Public Works 'tis his to sway,
With Mandate none dare disobey;
His place would suit me I opine,
I would John Hall's high lot were mine.

But stay he's not a happy man,
To please all parties he must plan!
The Super soothe, cajole colleagues,
And suffer other hard fatigues!

From the Super's whims he must keep clear,
And with his friends in office steer;
His Bills the Council may o'erhaul;
No! No! I would not be John Hall.

Sam Bealey's lot more pleaseth me;
He hath a handsome salary
To live in dignified repose,
While Hall and Rolleston prate and prose.

He has no nerve 'tis very true,
Bad to prevent, or good to do:
But as he hath no nerve, why he
Escapes responsibility.

Which way the Goldfield's road shall go,
He need not settle "Yes" or "No."
He's free to sleep if so inclined,
And never need make up his mind.

Yet Sam's is not a happy lot,
For he must stand the paper's shot;
Whose leaders, stinging and severe,
All with his bile may interfere.

And if the people's minds they jog,
The latter may tire of King Log;
If out their money they must fork,
They might prefer to have King Stork,

So when on Sam the papers fall,
I think I'd rather be John Hall;
But when Hall's budget's judged a flam,
Why then of course I would be Sam.

The Husband's Excuse.

MY dear, you reproach me for keeping your note,
Forgotten, for four or five days, in my coat;
But remember, my love, when you're railing the most,
That I never was made to be bored as a post.

R. T.

The Cur and the Calf.

IN the pleasant town of Christchurch not so long ago did dwell,
An actor, who, as actor's go, was something of a swell;
Caressed by gods and managers, he dwelt among the stars,
And everyone who heard him loved the rolling of his R's.

Full grave was his demeanour, as a tragic actor suits,
He stood six feet, or thereabouts, in rather high-heeled
boots.
A hat he wore with tragic slouch, and knickerbockers too,
As eminent tragedians occasionally do.

Since all men, whether streets they sweep, or senate houses
grace,
Have each their little weakness in some vulnerable place,
So, like a horse at auction that in vain a buyer begs,
Our hero's little weakness, to confess it, was—his legs.

In sooth they were a comely pair. O, would that such
were mine!
I'd wear a natty leathern shoe, and worsted hosen fine.
All gallantly I'd saunter round, or casually stand,
And envy ne'er a Bishop's calves in all this happy land.

One day, as all pre-occupied he strolled along the street,
He chanced upon a sleeping cur that, full of stolen meat,
With head and tongue and tail outstretched, lay dreaming
on the stones,
Pursuing visionary cats and gnawing phantom bones.

Unwary on the tail he trod, right heavily and fair;
The sort of thing you can't expect the mildest dog to bear.
So e'er the cur went flying from a well-directed kick,
One fatal bite had caught his leg and torn the hosen thick.

Yet haughtily our hero hied on in stately trim,
Unconscious of the stream that flowed adown the wounded
limb.
Till from the crowd a cad aloud exclaimed in tones of scorn
"Vy, Guvnor! vot's the matter with them patent legs
o' your'n?

He starts, he stops, he looketh round, he turneth ghastly
pale—
Along the pavement far he sees the sawdust's deadly trail.
One curse he gives, one bound he takes, he runs with
might and main,
And nevermore in Christchurch was that actor seen again.

Quite lately in Australia, among dramatic stars,
I met a tall man, given much to dwelling on his R's;
But I noticed he wore trousers, so cannot be the same
As one who several years ago was lost to Christchurch
fame.

R.

Reminiscences.

OH, the charms of a stroll in our nice little port,
When the crowds of new-comers are thronging ashore.
As we gaze on the victims our agent has caught,
We declare that we never can want any more!

" Ha, ha!" says a station man, raising his veil,
" There's a couple, they'll suit me exact to a hair;
" When they're settled a bit, I'll go up without fail,
" And engage them for fifty; that's lots for the pair."

And there jogs the farmer, who, six years ago,
Disconsolate landed with never a bob.
He is come from the plains for a bumpkin or two,
And looks a great swell on the back of his cob.

There's my lady, too, riding upon her grey mare—
The servant turned " Missis!" as big as you please.
" Oh, how wulgar," she minces, " Them ship people are;
" But I s'ppose I must have one in spite of the fleas."

And list to those gossips—" The good time is come,
  " And we've plenty: so lately in piteous case—
" They'll be only too glad, for a moderate sum,
  " To be nursemaid or cook, in our nice little place."

" All right," cries an old hand, who looks on the scene,
  " But I guess you will soon sing a different song;
" And those folks, who are certainly not very clean,
  " Though they're down in the mouth now, they won't be so long."

Ah, wizard! you've given the tables a turn;
  See, those whity-brown faces are flushing with pride;
And we're the poor folks who must wash, sweep, and churn,
  Or eat humble pie, as we stand by their side.

There's our sturdy up-country man down on his knees:
  Or at least, he's a look that he ought to be there.
" Oh, if fifty won't do, you may have what you please;
  " Only come for a little, and try what we are."

And our very fine lady, who must have a " gall,"
  Though I'm certain she'd really be better without—
" Will thirty, will forty pounds do, Miss? You shall
  " Have an evening whenever you like to go out."

And how do our poor simple gossips appear,
  As they range through the room not at all at their ease?
And 'mid a loud whisper of "What do they here?"
  Very humbly petition for help, "if you please."

" A cook's place," cries one, " Well, perhaps, it might do;
  " But you know I've been servant with forty and nine!
" Well, what do you give?" " Five-and-twenty for you,
  " Who are strong and can work hard." " Then I must decline."

" Five-and-twenty, indeed!" and she turned on her heel,
With a bounce that nigh frightened our gossips to fits.
" I suppose they don't think that *young ladies* can feel?
" And fancy we land here without any wits."

And what is the moral? Away with your tears!
Don the apron of freedom, and dust your own shelves!
Spend the wonderful wages on pin money, dears,
Leave the *ladies* alone, and be servants yourselves.

The Last Fly of Summer.

'TIS the last fly of Summer,
Left droning alone;
All his lively companions
Are frozen and gone.
No fly of his kindred,
No blue bottle's nigh,
That can tickle one's bald head,
Or fall in one's pie.

I'll not leave thee, thou lone one,
To pine on the pane!
Join thy wretched companions,
All frozen and slain!
Thus nimbly I seize thee,
And dash thee to ground;
Where thy mates of the ceiling
Lie trodden and drowned.

So peaceful I'll join in
Each meal of the day,
And bless the cold weather
That drives ye away.
If summers were constant,
And winters unknown,
Oh! who would live here,
To be always fly-blown?

Constable "E."

A True Story.

DEDICATED (WITHOUT PERMISSION) TO THE CHRISTCHURCH POLICE FORCE.

BRIGHT glittered the buttons of Constable E,
And bright was his intellect stated to be,
But dark were his whiskers, his uniform too,
And the tips of his finger-nails sable in hue,
And darker the looks from which criminals flee,
When darted upon them by Constable E.

One morning in autumn, a local inspector,
Head sergeant, detective, or other director,
Told Constable E. to betake himself down
To a nursery-garden not far from the town;
Whose owner complained that the larrikins near
Ne'er left him an apple, a peach, or a pear;
For what sparrow and moth uncorrupted left whole,
These thieves, as the Scriptures say, broke in and stole.

Our Constable's bosom swelled big at the thought,
"If I don't catch thim thaves it's meself should be coaart;
Though the owner's away it's not I'll be afraid,
If that nursery-garden a nursery-maid
Should contain, by the pow'rs 'twill be foiner, He! He!"
And he chuckled that gallant Hibernian E.

His uniform doffed, (whereat somewhat he sighed),
In a neat suit of tweeds to the orchard he hied:
Not a nursery-man, not a nursery-maid,
Not a thief nor his shadow the garden displayed:
Quoth he, as he stooped through the branches to push,
"Sure no Bobby before had his beat in a bush!"

But alas for our merry young catcher of thieves,
As he cautiously peered through an apple tree's leaves,
Something struck in his face, and he found as he rose
He had caught neat as ninepence a hook in his nose,
In an Irishman's face no appropriate thing,
Though Irish bulls wear them at times—or a ring.

Running-in was his art, and he'd done this so well,
No pickpocket ever caught easing a swell
Of his handkerchief, watch, or superfluous tin,
Had been, than the hook, more securely run in.
"Oh, I came on my own hook, and now it's on me!"
And he called—not on heaven—poor Constable E!

Now hard by the garden a dog did abide,
Who was loose in his ways, for he seldom was tied:
You'd own if awake on a midsummer night,
That his bark was, if possible, worse than his bite;
Though he never sat down, yet, a stranger to greet,
This singular dog often made for a seat.

So hearing E call on the devil and all,
The dog very properly answered the call;
And seeing a thief, as he thought, standing there,
Attacked him with zest in the flank and the rear,
Abetted therein by the gardener's boy,
Who aided the fun with such infinite joy
That he laughed till he cried in his culpable glee,
As "Take the daa-g aff now," yelled Constable E.

When a fish bites the hook, his condition is sad,
But at once to be bitten and hooked is too bad:
More rents in a minute on E did appear,
Than a landlord of Erin collects in a year;
He couldn't turn round with the hook in his nose,
And he couldn't stand still with the teeth in his clothes,
And what would have happened I'm puzzled to say,
When the packthread attached to the fishhook gave way.

What followed will never, I fancy, appear,
Since of dog nor of boy have I managed to hear;
How E got to town, too, I'd much like to know,
But this I *can* say: When he reached the depôt,
No man e'er looked muddier, bloodier, paler,
Or a goodlier subject for doctor or tailor.

Detectives who boast an adventurous vein,
In uniforms handsome or suits that are plain,
If you haven't a fancy for mud on your clothes,
One tail to your coat, and a hook in your nose,
If from dogs and disasters alike you'd be free,
Pray study the story of Constable E.

R.

Charlotte Godley's Well. (6)

THE packhorse wends his way,
From Lyttelton over the hill.
But oh! for that tank of the red red stone,
And a drink from that trickling rill!
Prate! Prate! Prate!
Of thy Public Works John Hall!
But that ruin of mud on the mountain side
Shall be type of thy speedy fall.

Oh, well for the stockdriver's cob,
For the creek where he quenches his thirst!
Oh, well, oh, well, for old Redman's Bob,
At the trough he may drink till he burst.
Prate! Prate! Prate!
Of thy Public Works, John Hall!
But the graceful gift of a friend that is gone,
Is none of thy care at all.

Song of the Cab-drivers.

(BY ONE OF THEMSELVES.)

OH! it's of the hackney carriages
 I'm going for to sing, sir;
We're licensed now for marriages,
 And all that sort of thing, sir.
The Council gives a character
 Unto each driving cabby;
And 'tis a certain fact, sir,
 We wouldn't cheat a babby.
  With my fol lol the cabby,
  And my fol-lol the ray!

This here is a four-wheeler neat,
 And there's my nobby Hansom.
There's other cabbies down the street,
 But you better hadn't chance 'em.
Look in, sir, here's the cleanest straw;
 You'll find the cushions dusted;
Oh! I'm a man what knows the law,
 And allays may be trusted.
  With my fol-lol the cabby,
  And his fol-lol the ray!

Hi! Cab, sir? Hi! now just step in:
 If you've business to transact, sir,
I'll drive you there, and back again,
 Accordin' to the Hact, sir.
The Council's fixed the fares, d'ye see,
 For plying round the city;
The Inspector's down on us, or he
 'll be sacked by the committee.
  With his fol-lol the cabby,
  And his fol-lol the ray!

But if mayhap you've just come down
  From some up-country station,
I'll drive you round and round the town,
  And guard you from temptation ;
And charge, per hour, ten bob at most ;
  And that's the lowest price, since
The Council's been and raised the cost
  By sticking on a license.
    With fol-lol the cabby,
    And their fol-lol the ray !

The law, its werry well, in course,
  For any other cabby,
What doesn't care to groom his horse,
  And turns out awful shabby.
But I don't want no law, not I,
  Nor Inspector's interference ;
You'd pick me, in a hundred, by
  My personal appearance.
    With my fol-lol the cabby,
    And my fol-lol the ray !

The Council at our money grabs,
  And makes us fork the fivers ;
They goes in now for moral cabs,
  And literary drivers.
And lor ! the law is awful tight,
  Down on all little larking ;
But mind, we doesn't find its bite
  For nothing like its barking.
    At the fol-lol the cabby,
    And the fol-lol the ray !

1865.

Commercial Summary for England.

OUR markets are extremely dull,
For trade is looking flat;
Merchants, more cautious than of late,
Are minding what they're at.

For discount interest is felt,
And cash is most unready;
But though the money market's TIGHT,
'Tis very firm and steady.

Fat cattle do not stir with ease,
As recent sales will prove;
And stations are quite station 'ry,
And difficult to move.

A moderate share of failures have
Occurred the month around,
With moderated dividends
Of nothing in the pound.

Bulk beer was strong all through the week,
Light ale is going out;
Porter clears off the market well;
There's heavy sale for stout.

The painful state of glass forbids
A look at it at all;
While frames and sashes run to waste,
And figure very small.

Best I. C. sugar now, I see,
Is estimated high;
Loaf's reached its very lowest point,
Crushed loaf doth lowly lie.

Old Tom creeps slowly out of store;
   Hops operate but badly;
Matches will not go off at all,
   And saddlery looks sadly.

Brandies of late some strength have shown;
   Rum holds a queerish place;
For whiskeys, spirit is displayed;
   But gin's in harder case.

For flour, wheat, oats, and other grain,
   Consumption shows decline;
For salt, large sellers fine have sold;
   The sale of coarse is fine.

For deals, the deals, the dealers say,
   Can scarcely show a line;
While birch is backward in demand,
   The sale of larch does pine.

Capers are lively; salmon dead;
   Rope hangs on hand too long;
Shipments of butter come in pat;
   And Cheshire cheese is strong.

Till prices rise, and failures fail,
   No cash the place can spare;
But all consignments still will have
   Our *unremitting* care.

A Leave-taking. (7)

THE seamen shout once and together,
   The anchor breaks up from the ground,
And the ship's head swings to the weather,
   To the wind and the sea swings round:

With a clamour the great sail steadies,
  In extreme of a storm scarce furled ;
Already a short wake eddies,
  And a furrow is cleft and curled
  To the right and left.

About me, light-hearted or aching,
  " Good-bye !" cry they all, taking hand—
What hand do I find worth taking ?
  What face as the face of the land ?
I will utter a farewell greater
  Than any of friends in ships—
I will leave on the forehead of Nature
  The seal of a kiss—let the lips
  Of a song do this.

We part from the earth, from our mother,
  Her bosom of milk and of sleep,
We deliver our lives to another,
  To cast them away or to keep.
Many-mooded and merciless daughter,
  Uncertain, strange, dangerous sea,
O tender and turbulent water!
  Make gentle thy strength, for in thee
  We put trust for a length.

Float out from the harbour and highland
  That hides all the region I know,
Let me look a last time on the island
  Well seen from the sea to the snow.
The lines of the ranges I follow,
  I travel the hills with my eyes,
For I know where they make a deep hollow,
  A valley of grass and the rise
  Of streams clearer than glass.

O what am I leaving behind me?
  No sorrow with tears for its debt—
No face that shall follow and find me—
  No friend to recall and regret—
Thought shall raise up the ghosts of some faces,
  But not of the faces of men.
A voice out of fair forest places
  Shall haunt me and call me, as when
  I dwelt by them all.

Now my days leave the soft silent byway,
  And clothed in a various sort,
In iron or gold, on the highway
  New feet shall succeed, or stop short:
Shod hard these may be, or made splendid,
  Fair and many, or evil and few,
But the going of bare feet has ended,
  Of naked feet set in the new
  Meadow grass sweet and wet.

I will long for the ways of soft walking,
  Grown tired of the dust and the glare,
And mute in the midst of much talking,
  Will pine for the silences rare;
Streets of peril and speech full of malice
  Will recall me the pastures and peace
Which gardened and guarded those valleys
  With grasses as high as the knees,
  Calm as high as the sky.

As the soul, were the body made regal,
  With pinions completed and light,
Majestic and swift as yon seagull,
  Even now would I take a quick flight,
And my spirit of singing deliver
  In the old hidden birthplace of song,
Sitting fast by the rapid young river
  With trees overarched, by no strong
  Sun or moon ever parched.

A singing place fitter than vessel
  Cold winds draw away to the sea,
Where many birds flutter and nestle
  And come near and wonder at me,
Where the bell-bird sets solitudes ringing:
  Many times I have heard and thrown down
My lyre in despair of all singing;
  For things lovely what word is a crown
  Like the song of a bird?

That haunt it too far for me wingless,
  And the hills of it sink out of sight,
Yet my thought were but broken and stringless,
  And the daylight of song were but night,
If I could not at will a winged dream let
  Lift me and take me and set
Me again by the trees and the streamlet;
  These leagues make a wide water, yet
  The whole world shall not hide.

For the island secure in my spirit
  At ease on its own ocean rides,
And Memory, a ship sailing near it,
  Shall float in with favouring tides,
Shall enter the harbours and land me
  To visit the gorges and heights
Whose aspects seemed once to command me,
  As queens by their charms command knights
  To achievements of arms.

And I will catch sight of their faces
  Through the dust of the lists and the din,
In the sword-lit and perilous places—
  Yea, whether I lose or I win,
I will look to them, all being over,
  Triumphant or trampled beneath,
I will turn'to the isle like a lover,
  To her evergreen brakes for a wreath,
  For a tear to her lakes.

The last of her now is a brightening
  Far fire in the forested hills,
The breeze as the night nears is heightening,
  The cordage draws tighter and thrills,
Like a horse that is spurred by the rider,
  The great vessel quivers and quails,
And passes the billows beside her,
  The fair wind is strong in her sails,
  She is lifted along.

When the zone and the latitude changes
  A welcome of white cliffs shall be,
I shall cease to be sad for white ranges
  Now lost in the night and the sea :—
But dipped deep in their clear flowing rivers
  As a chalice my spirit shall weigh
With fair water that flickers and shivers,
  Held up to the strong steady ray,
  To the sunlight of song.

FREDERICK NAPIER BROOME.

December, 1868.

The Doctors' Dilemma. (*)

AIR.—"The Vicar of Bray."

SCENE.—A patient's bedside in the Hospital.

Enter two PHYSICIANS.

First PHYSICIAN to second ditto—sings.

WHEN Officers of Health began,
  To cope with typhoid fever,
I vowed I'd ne'er report a case
  Of all that I took fee for.

His pulse is quick—his temperature
You need not record what the height is—
But if he dies, be sure you say
'Twas gastro-enteritis.

(Both.)

And this is true we will maintain
No matter what the right is;
That every sort of ache and pain
Is gastro-enteritis.

(To them enters third PHYSICIAN, examining the tongue of a Ligurian bee under a microscope.)

(Sings.)

This case I cannot recollect
Apart from other cases,
But still I am prepared to swear
There were no typhoid traces;
Phrenitis, in these far off lands,
May spring from typhoid sources;
And brains like tongues of bees may change
From "*climacteric*" causes.

CHORUS of three PHYSICIANS:

Then this is true, we will maintain,
That—if it's not phrenitis—
Then every sort of ache and pain
Is—gastro-enteritis.

(Enter fourth and fifth PHYSICIANS with attendants bearing on a stretcher the body of a man who has just fallen off the Cathedral tower.)

1ST PHYS.—A hopeless case—the skull is smashed.
2ND PHYS.—The brain is full of mortar.

3RD PHYS.—The neck is fractured, and the ribs
Forced in upon the aorta.
4TH PHYS.—The left leg—see—is crushed to pulp—
And nobody knows where the right is.
ALL ......—Mere trifles these—real cause of death
Was—gastro-enteritis.

CHORUS of five PHYSICIANS :

Then this is true, we will maintain,
That—if it's not phrenitis—
Then every sort of ache and pain
Is—GASTRO-ENTERITIS.

(Music Agitato. Enter CHORUS of UNBURIED GHOSTS flourishing death-certificates in their hands.)

GHOSTS singing :

Oh ! what shall we do
We can't get through
To the other side of Cocytus ;
And it's all along
Of your coming it strong
With your—gastro-enteritis.

FIRST GHOST—(solo).

I certainly died
Of something inside,
But *is "it rite" to enter*,
On this here ticket
Of leave to old Nick ; it
Was only a pain in my "venter." *

---

*For the benefit of the country gentlemen, as they say in the House of Commons, we will translate. *Gastro-enteritis* means a bad sort of stomach-ache. *Venter* is the Latin for stomach. The Ghost has evidently moved in polite Society, and shrinks from using the homely English word.

SECOND GHOST—(solo.)

And I quite disagrees
With that doctor of bees,
(Though he took his oath upon it)
That it's no matter what
A poor chap's got,
It's only a "bee in his bonnet."

CHORUS.

Oh! what shall we do, &c., &c.

Exeunt PHYSICIANS *pursued by* GHOSTS

F. W. H.

The Charge at Parihaka.

YET a league, yet a league
Yet a league onward,
Straight to the Maori Pah
Marched the Twelve Hundred.
"Forward the Volunteers!
Is there a man who fears?"
Over the ferny plain
Marched the Twelve Hundred!

"Forward!" the Colonel said;
Was there a man dismayed?
No, for the heroes knew
There was no danger.
Their's not to reckon why,
Their's not to bleed or die,
Their's but to trample by:
Each dauntless ranger!

Pressmen to right of them,
Pressmen to left of them,
Pressmen in front of them,
Chuckled and wondered.

Dreading their country's eyes,
Long was the search and wise,
Vain, for the pressmen five
Had, by a slight device,
  Foiled the Twelve Hundred.

Gleamed all their muskets bare,
Fright'ning the children there,
Heroes to do and dare,
Charging a village, while
  Maoridom wondered.
Plunged in potato fields,
Honour to hunger yields.
Te Whiti and Tohu
Bearing not swords or shields,
Questioned nor wondered,
Calmly before them sat;
  Faced the Twelve Hundred.

Children to right of them,
Children to left of them,
Women in front of them,
  Saw them and wondered;
Stormed at with jeer and groan,
Foiled by the five alone,
Never was trumpet blown
  O'er such a deed of arms.
Back with their captives three
Taken so gallantly,
  Rode the Twelve Hundred.

When can their glory fade?
Oh! the wild charge they made,
  New Zealand wondered
Whether each doughty soul,
Paid for the pigs he stole:
  Noble Twelve Hundred!

JANETTE.

A Lay of a Lost Spec. (*)

THERE stands a city on the plain by the South Pacific
shore,
A town as fair as any "City on the Plains" of yore:
To North and South, and East and West, its busy streets
extend
In strict and straight monotony, without a break or bend,
Save where, half way 'twixt Morten's huts and Warner's
Paphian bar,
The great Cathedral lifts its spire, a beacon from afar.
Dear to the heart of Mountfort is the sweet æsthetic spot
Where that tall tower proclaims to all how he "improved"
on Scott!
Dear to the heart of Lingard that dissonant refrain
When the ringers clang their discords out with all their
might and main:
Dear to the heart of Jacobs is that sweet and pious peal,
As from the holy fane the notes of "Annie Laurie" steal;
And dear to all good citizens that centre of their town,
Where each recurring tram reveals the form of Evans
Brown.

Yet is there one fair spot beside, within the city's ring,
Where more than all, of young and old, the fond affections
cling,
That wide expanse of verdant turf, those pleasant bosky
shades
Whose whispering boughs hear tender vows to timid love-
sick maids;
Where stalwart youngsters wield the bat; where o'er their
ashy round,
In all but utter naked grace Ollivier's athletes bound;
Where Armstrong, foe to lawless love, with mighty toil
and pain,
Is always planting trees by scores, and—cuts them down
again:

Where Harman of the iron will rules like a Southern Czar,
Save where the fishes own the sway of Frankish and of Farr.
Ah! Hagley Park, as oft at eve, on Avon's limpid tide,
By Worthy's classic lawns the laughter-laden wherries glide,
What soul so base as not to feel the magic of the scene,
And vow to keep thee free for aye, as thou hast ever been!

To this good town (I tell the tale as it was told to me)
Two strangers came, in days gone by, from o'er the rolling sea;
The first, a youthful Briton, brought from Albion's foggy shore
That cautious brain, that prudent mind, which always looked for "more:"
The second, grey, but lightsome yet, nursed 'neath the sun of France,
Still let no ardent warmth impel to losing of a chance.

They came, those noble beings, from the hot Australian sands,
Bearing hither priceless treasures, all the wealth of other lands,
Wishing, for the people's profit, all these wonders to display,
Wishing too, perhaps, some plunder for themselves to bear away.
'Tis sad to tell what conflicts stern befel this noble pair,
How Howland tried to drive them back, how Roberts grudged his Square.
In vain the wave of "progress" rose and drowned the feeble few,
And in the Park, 'neath Lambert's care, the fairy Palace grew.
In sooth it was a glorious pile, a too, too utter thing,
Where all the Graces, all the Arts, their beauties seemed to bring.

Four cloud-capped towers, majestic, were at each far corner placed,
The centre bore a lightsome arch, as if by angels traced;
And iron lent its rigid strength, and timber straight and trim,
And every wall was firmly braced with mighty sheets of scrim;
Hurrah! cried all the gazing crowd, what mortals can compare
With the stalwart might of Twopeny, the splendour of Joubert!

It boots not now to tell the tale, how, on an autumn day,
The city rose in festal guise, and all was grand and gay,
As the bright steel flashed, and the cymbals clashed, and the sullen cannon roared,
And the bells clanged out, and all the rout to the fairy Palace poured;
How all the hardy artisans paced the city through and through,
With forty men in nightshirts, and the butchers all in blue,
Nor must we tell how all the world in thousands thronged to fill
Those wondrous halls, and pour apace their shillings in the till.

The autumn days went swiftly by, and fate, whom all obey
Brought nearer still and nearer still the mournful closing day.
'Twas hard indeed to muse, dry eyed, upon that hastening time
When those two men, so great and good, must seek another clime.
'Twas sad to feel that soon no man would find a single trace,
Save rags and rubbish, dirt and straw, of all that glorious place:

And Joubert sighed to think how soon, when he was far away,
In the Park the girls would flirt again, the little children play.
His noble heart was touched with grief—he registered a vow—
And called to his assistance then his crony Ruddenklau.
He said, "Attend, my little friend, I have a little plan,
I want to get my money back for my building, if I can.
They have no souls, these Englishmen, their cold and narrow pride
Can only see themselves and shuts out all the world beside.
We came (myself and Twopeny) with a great and varied store,
We showed these petty bumpkins what they never saw before:
We showed them plates from Worcester, pots and jugs from far Japan,
Little Venuses from Italy, and Leda with her swan.
They've had the tight-rope gratis, entertainments small and big,
They've had the armless lady and the educated pig:
For them the Austrian Band has strummed the same tunes every day,
They've had Professor Bickerton and Carmini Morley's play—
And after all these wonders they won't even make a show
Of asking for our Palace as a keepsake when we go!
Now, on your chain of office, is it not hard mon cher?
Sapristi! if I knew the way, 'twould almost make me swear!"
"Mein frent," quoth little Ruddenklau, half weeping as he spoke,
"I do not know if what you say is earnest or in joke:
But you are right, for every way the case is hard, 'tis true,
And in my solid German soul I sympathise mit you.
We must forgive these English—they have not got der geist,
They won't be driven, like us, you know, but they may be enticed!

With them 'tis best to dangle some pretty, glittering lure,
And there's one or two would help I know, if we profit
could ensure.
Let Walton rouse the monied hive and whisper dividends,
Let Brown log-roll in Parliament, and work his little ends,
And I will speak when all your guests are primed with
good champagne,
And when the people hear their Mayor, they will not dare
complain."

The great day came, the Hall was filled, it was a sight to
see
Around those loaded tables such a glorious company!
There Joubert, playful innocent, in Wilson's tweeds arrayed,
Formed joyous contrast with his mate, so sombre, black and
staid;
There beamed, as if he seldom saw so many tempting
things,
The visage of our Speaker, sprung from Ireland's mythic
kings;
There clustered all those wise, good men, who, in their
country's cause,
And for their country's pay, consent to give their country
laws:
And Walton's foxy glance was there, and the hungry face
of Brown.
And on them all, from the canvas wall, the "Sirens" fair
looked down.

The feast is done: the joyous guests the sparkling goblets
drain,
The iron roof with din of loyal toasts resounds again:
Up stands Joubert—his bright eyes glare—he scents the
coming prey,
In plaintive tones he tells his tale and points his friends the
way.

He tells how all his noble work has cost him far too dear,
And Twopeny looks shyly down, and Walton drops a tear.
Then every guest with solemn mien sipped a little more champagne
As Ruddenklau in turn took up the melancholy strain.
"And shall it then be said of us in future times," he cried,
"That with a glimpse of fairy realms our hearts were satisfied?
Shall three short months suffice for us, of these transcendent halls,
Where every night brought new delight, from dolls to Fancy Balls?
What will remain if this grand pile should vanish into air,
To recall the form of Twopeny, the grace of Jules Joubert?
No, Gott bewahre! citizens, we have not sunk so low,
We'll keep them as mementos of our good friends when they go.

Some very honest gentlemen (their names withheld as yet)
A little lease of a little piece of Hagley Park shall get;
They shall buy this splendid building, and in this eternal Hall
They shall gaily fill their pockets and give pleasure to us all."
He ceased, but from the astonished guests came back no answering cheer,
No sound of warm approval rose to greet his anxious ear:
There was scarce one in all that room who did not feel afraid,
As every word revealed how well that subtle plot was laid:
Joubert looked grave, and Twopeny still at his plate gazed down,
And Brown looked hard at Walton, and Walton winked at Brown.

But when, next morn, the people heard how spoke that daring man,
At once through all the shuddering town a thrill of horror ran;

At once from all sides rose the cry of clamorous dissent,
'Till frightened Joubert vowed that nought but fun and joke was meant.
Nor, 'mid the din of protest, were our two great mentors mute,
The Tory print upheld the park, the Liberal followed suit.
So may it ever be, so may the people's wrath frustrate
Their plans who piecemeal would devour the people's fair estate:
And when the next base schemer on the Park shall make a raid,
May he be tarred and feathered, and may I be there to aid!

W. M. M.

NOTES.

(1.) "*Night-Watch Song of the Charlotte Jane.*"—The *Charlotte Jane* was one of the four ships which left England together, in September, 1850, conveying the first emigrants to Canterbury. Three of these ships arrived in Lyttelton harbour on the same day, December 16, 1850, though they had not sighted one another during the whole voyage from England. The *Charlotte Jane* was the first to drop anchor; and the *Sir George Seymour* and *Randolph* made their appearance within a few hours. The fourth ship, the *Cressy*, arrived after the lapse of a few days.

(2.) "*Pilgrims and Prophets.*"—During the first year of the Settlement, Canterbury was invaded by a body of Sheep-farmers from Port Philip (Victoria), who were regarded by the Settlers partly with admiration as successful colonists, and partly with horror as disbelievers in the art of colonization and the "Canterbury system." The visitors found the country admirably adapted for sheep-farming, and they treated with some contempt the raw emigrants from England who looked to agriculture as the foundation of their fortunes. One of the visitors, who seem to have delighted in the *soubriquet* of "Shagroons," ventured to prophesy, in a letter which found its way into print, that the "Canterbury Pilgrims" would soon be ruined, and their country left for occupation by his more enlightened comrades. The "pilgrims" sought no harsher revenge than to nick-name their Port Philip visitors "prophets," and to take example from their experience in pastoral pursuits. The Canterbury pasturage system was quickly adapted to the requirements of sheep-farming on a large scale, and "pilgrims" and "prophets" were soon merged into one class as Canterbury runholders.

(3.) "*Lines on a Recent Calamity.*"—Mr. William Deans, one of two brothers who settled at Riccartou, on the plains, long before Canterbury was founded, was drowned by the shipwreck of the vessel in which he was proceeding to Wellington, on his way to England, on the 23rd of July, 1851. Mr. Deans had been a warm friend to all classes among the Canterbury settlers.

(4.) "*The Shagroon's Lament.*"—One of the "Shagroons" from Port Philip entered upon the pastoral occupation of some country near the Gorge of the river Rakaia. There is, perhaps, no more windy spot in the whole of New Zealand, and the Shagroon did not long endure it. He quickly adopted the habits, occupation, and characteristics of a genuine "pilgrim," and now neither grumbles in verse nor prophesies in prose.

(5.) "*The Overseer's Lament.*"—Australia, not New Zealand, is the scene of the woes endured and described by the overseer.

(6.) "*Lay of the Last Registered Dog.*"—This song and the next—the "Proclamation"—were written at the time of the first election for the Superintendency, House of Representatives, and Provincial Council, in Canterbury, which took place at the end of the year 1853. Sir George Grey was then Governor of the Colony. The Candidates for the Superintendency were Mr. J. E. FitzGerald, who was successful, Mr. H. J. Tancred and Lieut.-Col. Campbell, who were defeated. "Ten Bob," used as the name of a dog, implies that the Registration Fee of Ten Shillings has been paid for him. [The references to Chinese and to Latin quotations are said to be explained by the following story. One of the candidates at this election was rash enough to make the importation of Chinese coolies a plank of his political platform. At an election meeting, a supporter of his introduced him to the free and independent as an expert in agriculture, saying:—Mr. —— is the man to tell you *Quis faciat lætas segetes, quo sidere terram, Vertere Mæcenas,* —— but the quotation was never finished for a stentorian voice from the crowd roared out "*No Chinese!*" and the second hexameter was drowned in a shout of laughter.]

(7.) "*Charades on Unpopular Subjects.*"—The "Unpopular Subjects" of the year 1856 were principally the means of communication through the country, and especially the North Road to Kaiapoi, the Lyttelton Bridle-path, and the ferries over the rivers.

(8.) "*Manuka Branches, with Holes between.*"—A practice was adopted for a short time of mending very bad holes in the road by throwing strong stakes and brushwood over the mud from side to side of the broken spot, and covering these with dry clay; by which means the road received the appearance rather than the reality of firmness.

(9.) "*What are the Customs Doing?*"—The Customs Tarriff was also an "unpopular subject" at the end of the year 1856, when the new principle was adopted of levying duties on some classes of imports by weight, and on others by measurement. A story goes that one of the first cargoes to arrive after the change consisted of cocoanuts, and that the Customs officials were driven to their wits' end to compute the duty payable upon each nut separately and the whole cargo collectively.

(10.) "*Our Beautiful Church is Tumbling Down.*"—Lyttelton Church was first built of brick, with timber framing, in the year 1852; but the building had to be taken down a few years afterwards. A substantial stone structure now occupies its place.

(11.)—*Lay of the Sumner Road*"—One of Mr. FitzGerald's last acts as Superintendent was to open formally the Sumner Road, by driving over it from Christchurch to Lyttelton. But several months before this feat was accomplished, the Superintendent invited all the Members of the Council to walk over the road, and form an opinion upon its merits. Opinions differed widely. Some persons thought that the Sumner line could never be rendered a serviceable dray road, and advocated the improvement of the Bridle-path for passengers, and the River for goods traffic, until the time for a railway should come. Others followed the opinion of the Government of the day, that a tramway through a high level tunnel under Evans Pass, on the line of the Sumner Road, would serve every present purpose, and even render a direct railway unnecessary for the future. The majority, however, seem to have come to the conclusion that an open road by Sumner, not turned into a tramway, and not passing through a tunnel, would be of great practical advantage for many years to come, and would be quite worth the money which must be expended upon it. The subject was one of daily discussion; opinions were warmly held, and not seldom violently expressed, for and against each scheme; and it needed but a small stretch of imagination to believe that the Members of Council who objected to the Sumner Road were ready to perish on the hated spot rather than abandon their principles. None of them did so; they visited the road, dined together at Sumner, abode by their previous views, and maintained the dispute actively for many following years.

(12.) "*Railroadior.*"—A proposal was made by the Provincial Government in the spring of 1856 to lay down a tramway from Lyttelton to Christchurch, on the line of the Sumner Road, passing under Evans Pass by a high level tunnel. This project, which is alluded to above, was not carried out.

(13.) "*Road Lines.*"—The Sumner line of tramway was to be combined with a common road, which was to be brought into use, while the tunnel should be in progress of construction, by means of steep zig-zags between the permanent line and the summit of Evans Pass. These zig-zags have been completed, and now form part of the Sumner Road.

(14.) "*The Town of Christchurch.*"—Christchurch, in 1857, was beginning to assume the appearance of a town. Cashel Street was the first which could boast of an almost continuous row of buildings on each side for a portion of its length. The Government offices and Council Chamber were accommodated in a house previously occupied by Mr. W. G. Brittan, between Cathedral Square and the river. The house was afterwards converted into an hotel, and has recently been pulled down in the progress of improvement. Readers of Irish song literature will not need to be told that the form of ballad in the text is a close imitation of the "Groves of Blarney" before that popular song was polished up—was it by Father Prout?—into regular metre and accurate rhyme. [But though the appearance of Christchurch in 1857 may have been impressive in the eyes of the Pilgrims, it had not always the same effect upon new comers. To them it was still "the city of magnificent distances." In that very year a gentleman, now well-known as an old identity, arrived for the first time in Lyttelton, whence, taking horse, he rode over the Bridle-path to visit the capital. Unawares he rode up High Street, through Cathedral Square, and along the Whately Road; and it was not until he had reached Papanui, that, suspecting he had lost his way, he enquired how much further it might be to Christchurch.]

(15.) "*Ballad of the Ancient Member.*"—The second Provincial Council of Canterbury was opened at the beginning of 1858. The first, under Mr. FitzGerald's Superintendency, had been presided over by several administrations or "Executives;" but none of the Ministers known to that Council were re-elected to the second, except Mr. Richard Packer and Mr. John Hall. [The gentlemen gingerly referred to by their initials in this ballad were Mr. Joseph Brittan, who in 1858 unsuccessfully contested the Superintendency with Mr. Moorhouse; Mr. Henry Sewell, whose prominence in the Canterbury Association naturally gave him a position in our Provincial Council, which his energy and debating talent fully sustained, and who is referred to later on in the "Song of the Squatters;" Mr. Cass, chief surveyor; Mr. W. J. W. Hamilton, then Collector of Customs, and afterwards for many years Receiver of Land Revenue; the Reverend William Aylmer, who subsequently settled at Akaroa; and Captain Simeon, at that time Resident Magistrate of Lyttelton, but who, after a not very long residence in Canterbury, returned to England and died there. Subsequent occupants of the Provincial "Chair," were the elder Mr. Charles Bowen, and Messrs. John Ollivier and H. J. Tancred."]

(16.) "*Song of the Squatters.*"—In the year 1858 the Land Regulations were altered by the Council, and some provisions respecting Pre-emptive rights on runs were introduced, giving, as many persons thought and still think, undue advantages to the run-holders. [*Oloware the fluent*, Mr. John Ollivier, one who has in his time played many parts, who just then was playing that of Provincial politician, and who now is filling the post of Resident Magistrate for Lyttelton. *Jonnioltok*, Mr., now Sir John Hall, then a squatter of squatters, and since reputed, although wrongly, to have been the originator of the "gridiron" system of land buying. *Scotje-tomsin*, Mr. Thomson's nickname, "Scotchy," was far better known than his baptismal appellation. *Bobirodi*, Mr. Robert Rhodes, then, though not now, a colossus among runholders. *Stunnem*, Mr. John Studholme, for many years a silent member of the Provincial Council and General Assembly. *Tomicas*, Mr.

Thomas Cass, an *ante* Pilgrim, one of our earliest Provincial Civil servants, and who if he had been monarch of all he surveyed, would have been despotic sovereign of no small part of Canterbury. *Old Suelli*, Mr. Henry Sewell, perhaps better known as connected with the General Assembly politics, than those of our Provincial Council, of which, however, he was one of the first elected members.]

(17.) "*The Sumner Road.*"—Captain Thomas, the Chief Surveyor and Engineer of the Canterbury Association, first laid out and partly constructed a line of road from Lyttelton to the Plains, by way of Evans Pass (the lowest saddle in the chain of hills) and Sumner. Under Mr. FitzGerald's Superintendency, Mr. Dobson, then Provincial Engineer, completed the construction of the road, but adopted a line differing considerably from that of Captain Thomas. When the road was first passable for a wheeled vehicle, Mr. FitzGerald drove a tandem cart along it from Christchurch to Lyttelton, and was received in the latter town with enthusiasm. Allusion is made in the text to the prison labour, by means of which that portion of the road nearest to Lyttelton was mainly constructed. During 1856 and 1857 one Alfred Ronnage was a notorious jail-bird, who was possessed of cunning enough to escape repeatedly from confinement, more than once by eluding the vigilance of the warder on the road works; but was never able to escape altogether. He was so desperate a character that the public were seized with a general terror whenever a fresh escape of Ronnage was announced. For each attempt Ronnage received an additional term of imprisonment, and it seemed that he would pass his lifetime in Lyttelton jail. He professed reformation at last, was on his best behaviour for a year, and was then allowed to leave the Colony.

(18.) "*Where's the Engineer?*"—Mr. Dobson, the Provincial Engineer, made an Exploring Expedition to the West Coast in the beginning of 1858. He was very much missed on the Eastern side of the Province, where the autumn and winter seasons happened to be excessively wet, and the roads became almost impassable in consequence. There was plenty of money in the Treasury at the time for all purposes; and the public chose to believe that the badness of the roads was due solely to the Engineer's neglect. But it is due to Mr. Dobson to say, that, even if his trip to the West Coast was a holiday excursion, no Government officer ever deserved one better, or made better use of it; for he completed a laborious and successful exploration of the Teremakau river, and the country dividing the head-waters of the Hurunui from the West Coast, and returned to Christchurch with many valuable additions to the topographical knowledge of the western territory of Canterbury.

(19.) "*The Nelson Appeal.*"—Nelson, in 1860, was the only gold-producing province in New Zealand. As one of the settlements founded by the New Zealand Company, that province was afflicted with "Company's Scrip"—namely, transferable orders, entitling the holder to so much waste land whenever and wherever (within the settlement) he might choose to take it. It was constantly desired and attempted by the Nelson people, through their Representatives in the Assembly, to have the "scrip" made available throughout the Middle Island, and not in the province of Nelson only; but the attempt, made for the last time in 1860, was defeated. At the same time, Nelson, which had a territory always inferior in extent and value to that of Otago or Canterbury, and had divested itself of the greater part of its estate by selling it cheaply, and therefore had little land fund, complained that it was required to pay an equal share with the other Middle Island Provinces of the New Zealand Company's debt, which had been charged exclusively upon the Middle Island lands. This complaint was listened to, and a new adjustment of the debt was made more favourable to Nelson. The epigram in the text has reference to the gold, the scrip, and the debt, in the historical sense here described.

(20.) "*The Town and The Torrent.*"—The possibility of Christchurch being overwhelmed by the waters of the Waimakariri has been asserted from the first settlement of the town. The river has done a great deal of damage at Kaiapoi; and the people of Christchurch have half expected to suffer similar disasters. The river has broken over its southern bank several times, and the escaping water has flowed down to the Avon, and through Christchurch, but no greater sign of its presence than the flooding of the latter river has been ever yet visible. On the occasion referred to in the text, an attempt was made to restrain the Waimakariri at the overflowing point, by constructing sheet piling along the edge of the bank for some distance; but the attempt was not successful. Mr. Dobson took advantage of the interest generally felt in the question to deliver a lecture upon it in Christchurch, which went to prove that any overflow at the dangerous spot must come down through the town. This opinion has since been confirmed with some modifications. For a long time after this lecture the river gave no trouble whatever; but recently (and notably on Christmas Day, 1865) there has been too much reason to doubt the "remarkable quietude of the Waimakariri."

(21.) "*Arcades Ambo.*"—Mr. FitzGerald returned from England in the year 1860, during Mr. Moorhouse's first tenure of office. [Mr. FitzGerald still occasionally pays Canterbury a visit from Wellington, where his official duties compel him to live; one of the last occasions of his doing so, was to walk as a mourner at Mr. Moorhouse's funeral, in Riccarton church-yard.]

(22.) "*The Lament of Canterbury.*"—[In 1862, when these lines were written, the root of all evil formed so much the staple of talk and speculation throughout the Colony, that the late Mr. Crosbie Ward used to declare that, soon New Zealand nurses would sing babies to sleep with the lullaby—

Gold, gold, fine bright gold,
Tuapeka, Wangapeka, bright red gold.]

(23.) "*The Lost Steamship.*"—The vessel referred to is the *City of Dunedin*, which was lost, with every one on board, a few hours after leaving Wellington Harbour for Nelson and Hokitika.

(24.) "*The Runaways.*"—The story of the escape of the Maori prisoners from Kawau is too well known to need repetition. But it may be remarked that "the same good-natured thing" has been done again. A number of Maori prisoners who were kept on board a hulk in Wellington Harbour managed to escape. Some perished and some were caught, but the greater part of them were never seen again. Mr. Titus White, who was in political charge of the prisoners on Kawau, and whose imaginary acts are described in the text, has since lost his life by the shipwreck or foundering of a schooner in which he was travelling from the Bay of Plenty to Auckland on Government service. [As the story of the escape will not, perhaps, be now generally remembered, it may be as well to repeat it. In 1864, about 200 Maori prisoners, mostly captured at the fall of Rangariri Pah, were sent to Auckland, and confined in the hulk *Marion*, lying in harbour there. Cooped up in this fashion, their health and spirits soon began to suffer, and Sir George Grey, then Governor of the Colony, had the hulk towed down to his island estate, Kawau, where they were landed and housed. They appear to have been employed in gardening, fencing, and so forth, but to have been left so completely unguarded that on September the 11th, 1864, there were only four Europeans with them. On that day therefore the Maoris, seized some boats belonging to the hulk, and rowed themselves over the mainland, distant only about two miles from Kawau. The day was Sunday, and their departure was only discovered by their absence from morning Church. H.M.S. *Falcon* was then lying off the island, but in a different bay—that in front of Sir George Grey's house. The runaways, after crossing successfully, established themselves on the top of a steep hill, Otamahua, where Mr. Titus White visited them and tried to induce them to return by dint of threats and promises. The Natives, however, were quite equal to the occasion and Mr. White's diplomacy effected nothing. Beside the Wellington escape above referred to, the reader may be reminded of the similar feat performed some years later at the Chatham Islands by the notorious Te Kooti.]

NOTES TO APPENDIX.

(1.) *The Session* was that held by the Provincial Council in the early part of 1865.

Cutting off Hospital Beer.—Mr. Rolleston was noted in those days for a laudable desire to make even the smallest savings in the public service; hence the chaff about not paying the charwoman, *ante* (the Adventures of Poor Cock Canterbury). If, in later days, Mr. Rolleston has learned to spend money liberally in other parts of the Colony, it must be set to his credit, that, where Canterbury is concerned, he still consistently adheres to his former rigid economy.

William Wilson.—Mr. Wilson, better known under his *soubriquet* of "Cabbage" (acquired from the nursery garden, of which he was formerly owner), is yet to be seen in Christchurch; and, though of diminished greatness, may still be heard, like one of Tennyson's horns of Elfland, "faintly blowing" of the wonderful pile and other things.

The Majors.—Messrs. T. White and A. Hornbrook.

Geraldine.—Mr. Alfred Cox, then member for that district.

Herr Tancred.—Mr. Henry John Tancred, at one time an officer in the Austrian army, now Chancellor of the New Zealand University.

Mr. Mark Pringle Stoddart, who as may be seen in the early pages of this book, was not only, as here, the cause of rhyme in others, will be well remembered by all old settlers in the neighbourhood of Lyttelton Harbour, as an enthusiast in the cause of acclimatisation.

(2.) This clever bit of verse making, evidently the work of Mr. Ward, was written by way of a good humoured revenge for much fault finding with Canterbury and all belonging to it. Mr. Louis, who had a full share of a lawyer's instinct for detecting real or imaginary flaws, was a voluminous correspondent of the morning papers of the day, and few of our laws, bye laws, customs, or institutions escaped his dolorous criticisms.

(3) The road was that about to be made through the Otira Gorge to connect Canterbury and Westland, and which it was vainly hoped would prevent the latter district from breaking away from the parent province. Mr. Samuel Bealey, who, between Mr. Moorhouse's second and third term of office, was Superintendent, had for his Provincial Secretary in 1864-65 Mr. William Rolleston, then a young politician, who, with Mr. John Hall, were supposed to have Mr. Bealey in leading strings, and the attacks upon these three in the Canterbury *Punch*, from which this, and several later rhymes, are taken, were more humorous than merciful.

The reader who has the patience and time to consult the Appendices to the Journals of the House of Representatives of 1864-65, will find that though Governor Grey may have had "little to say" to Mr. Weld, he had plenty to write. The correspondence between His Excellency and his ministers is not wanting in vigour.

(4) Mr. George Sale, now Professor of Classics at the Otago University, was at that time a warden in Westland.

Mr. William White, in spite of the asseverations here put into his month, did not complete his tramway to Little River. He did, however, build bridges over the Waimakariri and Rakaia, and was concerned in other public contracts. His son, Mr. W. White, jun., is now M.H.R. for Sydenham.

(5.) In May, 1865, the first sod of the railway which now connects Christchurch with the Bluff, was turned. Shortly afterwards, Mr. Rolleston resigned the post of Provincial Secretary, and retired from the Executive Council, as his views on the policy of developing Canterbury by railway extension did not agree with those of his colleagues. Mr. Rolleston, in fact, considered the starting of the Great Southern Railway, as it was called, very inopportune. A caricature published in the *Canterbury Punch* of that date depicts Mr. Rolleston driving resolutely off in his solitary donkey cart, while his former companions, Messrs. Bealey and Hall, are mounting a locomotive engine driven by Mr. Sefton Moorhouse.

(6.) Little is now (1883) left of the "graceful gift" erected by Mrs. Godley on the Bridle-path between Christchurch and Lyttelton. The cross has fallen and been stolen or removed, and the well is almost hidden by stones and earth on which grass is growing. The statue standing to Mr. Godley in Cathedral Square contrasts strangely with the neglect with which his wife's present has been treated.

(7.) "*A Leave-taking.*"—Mr. Broome, now Governor of Western Australia, took his leave of us in December, 1868. This poem was written and published just previous to his going on ship-board. The hills referred to in the verses are presumably those of Malvern, where Mr. Broome's station was, and where his wife, Lady Barker, lays the scene of most of her amusing book "Station Life in Canterbury, New Zealand."

(8.) "*The Doctors' Dilemma.*"—This poem refers to a medical dispute, between the Health authorities and the physicians of the Christchurch Hospital. It appears that it is compulsory on the medical men in charge of an infectious case to notify the same to the Health authorities. It was asserted that the physicians of the Hospital did not do this with regard to typhoid fever, but concealed such cases under the name of gastro-enteritis, or inflammation of the stomach and intestines. A Government Commission was appointed to investigate the matter, and since then gastro-enteritis has ceased to appear amongst the fatal diseases of the Christchurch Hospital, and typhoid or enteric fever has taken its place.

(9.) "*A Lay of a Lost Spec.*"—Whether Messrs. Joubert and Twopeny's Exhibition really was a lost spec for its promoters, was, at the time when this lay was written, the subject of quite a lively little controversy. M. Joubert, who ought to have known, declared that it was, and published a balance sheet which bore him out. Against this it was roundly declared that the balance sheet was incomplete, and formed but another instance of the truth that there is nothing so misleading as figures. It was alleged that M. Joubert had left out of his calculations the value of the Exhibition building, at that time still standing, and a rhymester addressed, in one of the daily papers, an effusion to M. Joubert, the first verse of which ran :—

"Believe me if all those endearing old barns,
Which I gaze on so fondly to-day,
Were disposed of by means of some auctioneer's charms,
Demolished, and carted away,
The sweet sense of profit should soften the smart,
At least so it seemeth to me,
A Snug little balance on Twopeny's part
And a *Soupçon* my Joubert for thee.

M. Joubert's object in representing his affairs as unfortunate was supposed to be a desire to induce the Municipality in pity to purchase his building at a good figure and convert it into a public hall of some sort. It only remains in fairness to say that though this design was shortly nipped in the bud, there unhappily appears no doubt that the Exhibition's enterprising promoters reaped something less than no reward at all for their plucky speculation. The Exhibition formed a very pleasant resort for townspeople in the winter months of 1882, and though some of its features had perhaps grown almost as monotonous as the tunes played by the Austrian band, its disappearance left a gap in the town's amusements which has not yet been filled.

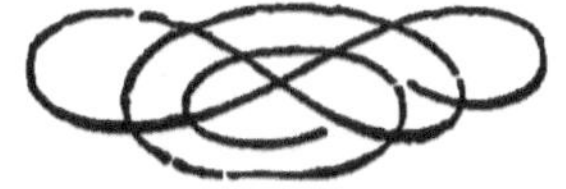

www.ingramcontent.com/pod-product-compliance
Lightning Source LLC
Chambersburg PA
CBHW031122020726
47495CB00007B/2310
* 9 7 8 3 3 3 7 2 5 9 6 3 1 *